DEAD
HILL

**A gripping murder mystery featuring Detective
Chief Inspector Jack Harris**

JOHN DEAN

THE
BOOK
FOLKS

Paperback published by The Book Folks

London, 2017

ISBN 978-1-5209-2575-2

www.thebookfolks.com

And this is where he comes. The place where he finds peace. The place where his demons cease their chatter. The place where he is at one with his world. At least for a few snatched hours.

Chapter one

The man saw him fall. The man knew why he fell. The man heard his sigh as he stumbled and threw up an arm before pitching forwards to hit the ground. The man glanced round the abandoned quarry to see if anyone else had seen it happen. Satisfied that he was alone, he stared down at the lifeless body with an expression of satisfaction and his face creased into a smile. Finally it was done. It was at an end. Dead Hill had claimed another one of its own. After a few seconds, the man turned and walked briskly out across the windswept fell. Soon the gathering mists swallowed him up. It was as if he had never been there.

'Come on,' murmured Jack Harris, scanning the hillside with his binoculars. 'I know you're up there.'

The detective chief inspector squinted in the bright late-afternoon sunshine as he tried to pick out the tiny specks that had been steadily working their way down off the fells for the best part of two hours. Standing on the edge of a copse half way up the hill, he had been watching them since shortly after three, his first glimpse having come as they emerged on the ridge, silhouetted against the horizon. It had taken him a while to spot the tiny shapes picking their way across the skyline but, once he had the men in his sights, the detective followed their progress intently. Occasionally he would lose sight of them when scudding clouds blotted out the sun, sending long shadows snaking across the slopes. But his concern did not last long, the men reappearing as the sun re-emerged. Each time, Jack Harris would give a sigh of relief. He did not want to lose them now.

Although unwelcome, the gang's presence on Dead Hill was not a surprise. That they had made their journey north was inevitable, even though they knew there was every chance that they would run into him. With nothing to do but watch and wait, Harris reflected on how he had been warning anyone who would listen that the force needed to take action to prevent the men committing the outrage on its patch. Even if the top brass did not share his passion for protecting the golden eagles, then at least they should act to prevent a public relations disaster. 'Think of the headlines,' Harris had said angrily, banging his fist on the table and earning himself a stern rebuke from Superintendent Curtis. As so often in his dealings with the commander, the inspector's words fell on deaf ears, the senior officer blandly citing 'budgetary restrictions' and 'different priorities' but never meeting the DCI's gaze as he rejected the call for extra manpower. Harris had stormed from the room.

'Bloody fool,' said Harris loudly, then instinctively glanced round as his words seem to reverberate round the copse.

But he knew that there was no one to hear his frustration. Story of his life as a police officer, he told himself bitterly. Accompanied by such dark thoughts, Harris resumed his lonely vigil, watching silently as the men picked their way down the higher slopes of Dead Hill.

The story had begun some weeks before when a wandering eagle, a male heading south from the Scottish Borders in search of a new territory, had looked down through the rain sweeping the North Pennines. Spying the female perched on a narrow ledge in an abandoned quarry, the male had swooped low over the fell and, in time, nature took its course. The realisation that the female was incubating eggs excited the local bird-watching community: it would be the first time golden eagles had bred in that part of the country for nearly a century.

Although everyone tried to keep the news secret until the chicks hatched, it was not long before the event attracted the illegal egg collectors, lured north by the grand prize. And it was a grand prize: rarity brought value on the black market and Harris had heard talk of several thousand pounds being offered by an unnamed London collector. To prepare for the thieves' arrival, volunteers with the local raptor protection group, Jack Harris among them, had given up every spare hour to provide a round-the-clock guard on the nest. Through hail and snow, rain and gale, they had watched, but what they had really needed, Harris had argued, was police support and a commitment to stop known illegal collectors when they ventured into the division. He had even supplied a list of names and car registration numbers.

The support had not been forthcoming and the telephone call to Harris that Wednesday afternoon had shattered his hopes. The call arrived when the detective chief inspector was in one of the interview rooms at divisional headquarters, a rambling Victorian house just off the market place in the little hill town of Levton Bridge. He had been trying to keep his temper as he interviewed a local youth suspected of breaking into a shed in the garden behind the town's post office. Headquarters were having a much-publicised drive against burglaries and all detectives had been told to focus on the offences to the exclusion of just about everything else. Harris was generally loathe to involve himself in such matters – there might not be much serious crime in the division to keep him busy but, as head of CID, he knew that shed-breaks were far beneath him. However, with his detective inspector on annual leave, his political instinct told him that showing willing was the thing to do on this occasion, so he had amazed his team by offering to make the arrest and conduct the questioning. It would, he reasoned, play well with Curtis, if nothing else. Might even persuade him to change his mind about the eagles.

Sitting in the interview room, Harris had spent an hour regretting the decision: he knew the scroat had screwed the place, the scroat knew he knew and the DCI was rapidly tiring of the 19-year-old's irritating smirk. More than once, Harris had bunched his fist beneath the table. Anger management, he reminded himself, anger management. With Harris becoming more and more frustrated, it came as a relief to policeman and suspect alike when they were disturbed by the uniformed officer. The DCI's relief did not last long. On hearing the phone caller's name – George Carroll was a park ranger and the leader of the raptor group – Harris had sprinted down the corridor to his office and snatched up the telephone, listening grimly for a moment before slamming the receiver down and grabbing his coat. He rushed into the CID squad room, ordered one of his startled team to take over the interview then thundered down the station corridors – he was a big man – and out into the car park.

Squeezing his white police Land Rover past the patrol cars and vans, he edged out into the busy market place, sounding his horn to part the shoppers. Having reached the edge of town after a couple of minutes, Harris had sworn when his progress was blocked by a farmer driving his red Fiat slowly down the hill, all white knuckles and staring eyes. Cursing, the DCI had put on his blue light and siren and veered round the car, causing the old fellow to swerve and come perilously close to clipping a parked van. Harris did not even glance back to check that he was alright.

Harris had driven furiously along the winding roads for twenty-five minutes, initially snapping orders into his radio then lapsing into a grim silence as he hurled the vehicle round the tight bends, oblivious to the moorland vistas that had opened up on either side of him. Geordie Carroll had said on the phone that he had spotted three men leaving the quarry. Three men.

As the springtime sun started to descend, the detective chief inspector left his hiding place and walked slowly along a rough track to stand behind a drystone wall a little further up the hill. Old habits dying hard, he made the ascent cautiously because, even though on arrival at the hill he had changed from his dark suit into a green T-shirt, camouflage jacket and brown trousers, he knew that any sudden movement would still be seen from above. It took him fifteen minutes to walk to his new position. Harris glanced back down the slope and gave a grunt of satisfaction; his Land Rover, which he had backed into the copse on his arrival, remained concealed from view, even from someone with the advantage of height.

He crouched behind the wall and looked up through his binoculars once more. It had, at times, been difficult to keep the trio in sight, particularly with the now fading light. Harris was not too worried: he had grown up in this area and knew every inch of the fell from childhood wanderings. And since returning to work for the police in the area some years previously, he had walked many more miles on the hills, accompanied as ever by Scoot, a black Labrador currently sitting silently in the back of the Land Rover, waiting patiently for his master's return. Superintendent Curtis objected to the animal's presence during work hours, and had banned him from Levton Bridge Police Station within days of taking up his posting as divisional commander in 2005. However, the inspector's brooding silence and protests from other officers, who enjoyed feeding the animal titbits from their lunchboxes, had forced Curtis to relent. He had done so reluctantly and had not forgotten his embarrassment during the three years that had followed.

The detective chief inspector scanned the hillside again but could not see the men. He guessed that, having crossed the boggy area as they came off the fell, they would be picking their way carefully down the footpath along the gully through which danced and chuckled the beck, swollen and flecked with the winter rains. It was impossible to see them from where he was standing, and to edge any further round risked giving himself away, but Harris suspected that the men might even have reached the bottom of the gully by now and sought the cover of the rocky outcrop known to local people as Parson's Nose. He guessed the men would be sheltering to catch breath after their exertions.

Harris reasoned that, ever cautious, they would glance down at their vehicle in the car park at the bottom of the hill; it had not taken the DCI long to confirm that it belonged, as expected, to Liverpudlian Eddy Rawmarsh, a villain with convictions for auto-crime, theft and handling stolen goods stretching back many years, as well as three for illegal egg collecting, two in Scotland and one in Cornwall. Harris knew that unlike those collectors who were driven by obsession, Eddy Rawmarsh was in it for the money.

The detective chief inspector knew, because his vehicle was parked next to that of Rawmarsh, that one of the men with him was the boorish Paul de Luca, who lived in Manchester and was a known criminal associate of Eddy Rawmarsh. Not that Harris needed telling about Paul de Luca. They went way back. Way, way back. Harris knew that de Luca would be there to provide the hired muscle should they encounter trouble: anything for a few quid, Paul de Luca.

Harris assumed that the third man was Gerald Hopson, the odd one out, a bespectacled financial advisor who lived and worked in London. Harris knew why he was there: Hopson was the expert, the one who understood birds. Hopson's criminal record was clean: he had even managed to evade justice for egg collecting the previous year when he, Rawmarsh and de Luca were found not guilty by magistrates in Shrewsbury. There had been unconfirmed rumours that de Luca had threatened the main witness, a woman who had seen the men near the nest when she was out walking her dog. Whatever the truth of the gossip, the woman did not appear on the day of the hearing and the case collapsed.

The thought only served to sharpen the inspector's appetite for the impending confrontation with the men on Dead Hill. He speculated that, on seeing the lower slopes deserted apart from grazing sheep, they might allow themselves a smile of triumph. Perhaps they would shake hands, anticipating the adulation that awaited them when word spread around the underground network of egg collectors. Harris guessed that, having assured themselves that they were safe, they would leave the outcrop to start, with light step, on the final short walk across the fields and down to the car park. That was when Jack Harris would strike. He had decided to wait; there was no point walking up to meet them. There would be no restoring the eggs to their parents now, the damage had been done, the eggs would be cold, the chicks perished. All that awaited was for Harris to take his revenge on the men. Without realising it, the inspector clenched his right fist, almost dropping the binoculars.

'Now, now,' he murmured. 'Behave yourself.'

Surveying the scene from above, the man knew he would enjoy the confrontation as well. Concealed behind a large rock high above them on the ridge, he also had been watching the collectors' descent, allowing himself a thin smile as he heard them cursing when they sank in up to their knees at one point.

'Bloody townies,' he had muttered, laughing at his own joke.

Crouching low to avoid being spotted by the detective chief inspector down below, the man could see the men clearly through his binoculars as they paused behind the rocky outcrop. He glanced down at Jack Harris, who was exhibiting signs of restless energy. A smile played on the man's lips: the confrontation was inevitable. It would make for good sport.

Harris cursed as, leaning his elbows on the wall, he scanned the hillside once more. It was twenty minutes since he had seen the men.

'Come on,' he said.

Moving swiftly and silently, a legacy of his Army training, Harris hurdled the wall and sprinted across the field, keeping low then crouching behind one of the ramshackle little stone barns that littered the landscape. Satisfied that his hiding place afforded him a better view without risk of detection, Harris straightened up and raised his binoculars. He had to scan the slopes for a minute or so before he caught sight of the men working their way with quickening step along the footpath through the fields. They were no more than 200 metres from him.

'Come to daddy,' he said, allowing himself a rare smile which faded as they clambered over the stile leading into his field. 'Damn, it *is* two.'

Harris had been wrestling with the problem for some time. He had only ever seen two figures during the descent. Because the men had been strung out, he had not been too concerned: he had assumed that the one with the eggs was lagging behind because of his delicate cargo. Broken eggs were of no value to anyone. All the available intelligence had suggested the three of them would come north together, and Geordie Carroll had seen three men in the quarry. Harris had not questioned the fact but now there could be no doubt that one of the men was missing.

He rapidly ranged across the higher reaches of the slopes with his binoculars to see if the third one had fallen behind but there was no one else. For just a second, his gaze settled on a large rock on the ridge. It seemed, just for a fleeting moment, as if something had glinted in the fading afternoon sun. He peered closer; could he detect movement? Was it de Luca? He saw nothing but it disturbed him all the same. He returned his attention to the two men in the field then glanced down to the car park at the bottom of the hill, reached into his coat pocket and brought out a radio.

'Matty,' he said to his detective sergeant, who, with two uniformed officers, was crouching out of sight behind the car park's toilet block, 'you in position?'

'Sure am.'

'Well, there's something wrong.'

'Too true,' said Gallagher's disembodied voice. 'I've just stood in a puddle. My shoes are ruined. I only got them last week. They're Ital...'

'Forget your bloody shoes! There's only two of them coming down.'

'So maybe only two of them went up,' said Gallagher.

'No, Geordie Carroll was adamant. Three.'

'Maybe he's wrong.'

'Don't think so. He was in Army surveillance.'

'That's alright then.'

'Those lads are never wrong.'

'So one of them went home a different way.'

'This isn't a WI outing,' snapped Harris. 'These guys don't stop to smell the flowers.'

'Whatever.'

Matty Gallagher was doing little to conceal the fact that the whole affair was boring him and had been from the outset and, without realising it, the sergeant had strayed briefly into the inspector's view.

'Get back!' snapped Harris, watching him through his binoculars, 'and don't hold the phone away from your ear when you're talking to me.'

Gallagher started and clapped the phone back to his ear.

'So what do we do now?' he asked, trying to sound more respectful.

11

'We need to find out what's happened and we need to find out now.'

'Remember what we said,' cautioned Gallagher, recognising the inspector's change in tone. 'Let them come down to me and the boys. No heroics.'

'There won't be any bother, not with these jokers.'

'Yes, but de Luca's a nasty piece of work and… guv?'

Gallagher reached quickly for the binoculars being held by one of the uniforms and scanned the hillside just in time to see Harris step out onto the path.

'Marvellous,' sighed Gallagher. 'Rambo's at it again.'

He and the uniforms started to run across the car park. Harris saw them moving and smiled: it would all be done and dusted by the time they arrived. He turned his attention back to the footpath and the approaching men.

'Well, well, well,' said Eddy Rawmarsh as he and Hopson came to a halt within a few feet of the waiting inspector, 'and what brings you here, pray?'

Harris surveyed him with distaste. Rawmarsh was in his late-forties, a wiry man with sallow cheeks and greasy brown hair, matted with sweat from his exertions. He was wearing a flat cap, a Barbour jacket and mud-flecked jeans and Harris noted that his walking boots were wet, but, for all his dishevelled appearance, there was a cool assurance about Rawmarsh's demeanour.

Gerald Hopson, standing a few paces behind Rawmarsh, did not exude such confidence. Aged in his early fifties and overweight, he was perspiring profusely from the descent, his pudgy face red and his balding pate glistening with sweat. Dressed in a dark blue designer windcheater and green cords, he eyed the detective inspector nervously. Harris knew that, unlike Rawmarsh, Hopson's encounters with the police always left him uneasy. Not that it had ever stopped him heading back to the hills. And if there was such a big price on these particular eggs…

'Where's your pal?' asked the chief inspector, seeing the path still empty behind the men.

'What pal?' said Rawmarsh.

'Don't play games. Where's Paul de Luca? I knew he was with you –
you were seen.'

'Yeah, well whoever said that was mistaken, we've been alone all day,' said Rawmarsh, clicking his fingers as if a thought had suddenly struck him, and turning round to look at Hopson. 'Come to think of it, we did meet a bloke out walking, didn't we?'

'Yeah,' said Hopson, nodding furiously. 'Must have walked with him for a couple of miles.'

'Did you get a name?'

'We weren't with him that long,' said Rawmarsh. 'He turned off onto another path. Last thing we saw he was heading over towards Hellens Wood.'

'What did he look like?'

'Average,' said Rawmarsh blandly. 'Nothing special.'

'What colour was his hair?'

'He had a hat on.'

'What colour?'

'Blue. Sorry, Harris, we're not being much help.'

The detective surveyed him for a few moments. He knew that Eddy Rawmarsh was an accomplished liar but could he be telling the truth this time? Could Geordie Carroll be mistaken? Carroll did say he was some distance away at the time and didn't get much of a look at the men. Rawmarsh, who seemed to enjoy the policeman's hesitation, winked at Gerald Hopson. Harris saw the gesture and scowled.

'So, what were you doing up here?' he asked curtly.

'Just out for a nice little walk,' said Rawmarsh.

Hopson gave a girlish giggle but glanced away when Harris glared at him.

'Well, you're a long way from home,' said the DCI, gesturing down the hill. 'Shall we?'

Rawmarsh followed the detective's gaze and calmly surveyed Gallagher and the two uniforms struggling up the slope.

'And if we decline your kind offer?' he asked.

Harris let his eyes range back up the hill where he noticed a light fog starting to roll gently across the ridge. He knew that sight. Had seen it many times down the years. It may only be wisps now but give it a couple of hours and it would be as thick as a blanket. He doubted there would much chance of mounting a search for Paul de Luca that late in the day.

'Listen, Eddy,' said the inspector, and there was an urgency in his voice, 'if your mate gets lost in that fog, there's every chance...'

'Like I said, we don't know anything about de Luca,' and Rawmarsh gave a slight smile. 'Maybe you should stick to shed burglaries. I hear there's been a spate of them in Levton Bridge.'

Jack Harris looked at him bleakly. It was as if the superintendent was talking.

Chapter two

'This is just too dangerous,' said Bob Crowther as he stood half way up Dead Hill and listened to the roaring silence of the night. 'I can't risk anything happening to any of the lads.'

Sitting on a rock and peering through the swirling fog at the looming shape of the hill above him, Jack Harris nodded. It was shortly after seven thirty and the mountain search and rescue team had been battling their way up the slopes for the best part of an hour. It had been a tortuous journey, the dozen volunteers continually slipping and sliding as they attempted to haul themselves up the muddy track, the mist thickening with every step that they took. On many occasions, Crowther had paused to stand and stare into the murk, feeling the isolation and disorientation that always came with fog. Not usually a poetic man, Crowther had often said that no one had ever truly experienced loneliness until they stood amid the northern hills when the fog had rolled in. He felt that loneliness now and his thoughts returned time and time again to the man they believed to still be up there.

Crowther had every reason to respect Dead Hill: as leader of the volunteers for a decade he knew only too well the way the uplands could suddenly change their mood, switching rapidly from reassuring sunshine to dankness and gloom as they claimed the unwitting walker. As a veteran of more than a hundred rescues, Bob Crowther had brought down a dozen bodies and each one had felt like a defeat, a loss that was deeply personal. But he also knew that there were times when you had to admit defeat, and that once the team crested the hill and stepped out onto the fells, they would be entering a world scattered with hidden shafts, the legacy of the area's 19th Century lead mining industry. Crowther glanced back down the slope and saw the indistinct shapes of his men trudging up the track.

'Even if we get to the top,' he said, 'we'd never see the shafts. Not in this.'

'So what are you saying? Call it off?'

'We have to.'

The inspector, himself a team member for eight years, surveyed his friend for a few seconds.

'And have you ever done that?' he asked.

'Once. Before your time. Never did find the poor bastard.'

'I assume you mean Jimmy Roscoe.'

'Jimmy Roscoe,' said Crowther, with a nod.

The inspector looked up at the hill again.

'Your call, Bob,' he said. 'I'll back you whatever you decide.'

Crowther waited for the remainder of his team to join him, the only sound the clanking of their equipment and the heavy trudge of their boots. They gathered around him, breathing hard after their climb, and looked at him expectantly.

'I am going to call it off,' he said.

The volunteers watched him in silence, the difficulty of their predicament etched in all their faces. Eventually, his deputy Mike Ganton, a tall grey-haired man in his mid-fifties, voiced the thoughts of the others.

'But what if he's up still there, Bob?' he asked.

'There's no way we can get to him,' said Crowther, gesturing at the fog. 'Not in this. We have to think of our safety as well.'

'God be with him then,' said Ganton and crossed himself.

* * *

Clouds as dark as the inspector's mood hung over the northern fells the next day as he stood in sombre silence and surveyed the broken body sprawled on the floor of the old quarry.

'So he was up here,' said Crowther quietly, looking at the man's swarthy face.

Everyone knew Paul de Luca.

It was late morning and they were in the far corner of the quarry, which had been abandoned when the workings came to an end twenty years previously. It had stood silent and empty ever since the men walked off the job for the last time, gradually being taken over by the sprawling vegetation. Tools lay where they had been dropped and there were rusting pieces of equipment propped up against a ramshackle corrugated iron shed near the entrance, its walls buckled and the roof long since caved in by a rock fall one winter afternoon. Anyone peeking through the door, which hung precariously from a single hinge, would see tea mugs and an old rusting metal lunchbox. Some walkers had even suggested that the quarry was haunted by the ghosts of the men who had died there down the decades, caught in rockfalls as they hewed at the cliffside. Jack Harris and Bob Crowther had no time for such superstitious thoughts as they stood and stared at de Luca in silence.

Certain it had been the correct call the previous evening, Crowther had nevertheless slept little that night and was up early the next morning, sitting in his kitchen long before daylight, map spread out on the table, and sipping a mug of tea as he planned the day's operation.

Despite all his preparation, it had still taken the searchers several hours to find what they were looking for. Having failed to locate Paul de Luca along the many narrow paths that criss-crossed the fell, they had entered the quarry shortly before eleven, where they found him lying at the base of the cliff, right leg twisted awkwardly, curly black hair matted with dried blood, jeans and windcheater torn and caked with dirt. It was Bob Crowther, clambering over a boulder in the lee of the cliff, who had stumbled upon the corpse, his cry bringing Jack Harris running. Now, Crowther stood and looked down at the inspector, who was still crouched down as he continued his examination of the body.

'You look puzzled,' said Harris, glancing up at him.

'It just doesn't look right, Hawk.'

Jack Harris had been known as Hawk ever since his love of wild birds became common knowledge as a schoolboy at Levton Bridge Primary. It had been a scrawny little chap in short trousers, himself revelling in the nickname Ferret, who had chosen Jack's monicker. Harris, Harris Hawk, Hawk, he had announced gleefully to his friends one day in the playground, and the name had stuck.

'What doesn't look right?' said Harris, straightening up.

'It's almost like somebody dragged him there.'

'Maybe they did,' said Harris, noticing one of the eagles circling high above, surveying them with beady eyes. 'And what did you see, my friend?'

Crowther flicked up the hood of his orange kagoul as the rain started to fall harder.

'Do you reckon he was alive last night?' he asked, rubbing his beard nervously. 'I'd hate to think that we left a dying man out here alone, Hawk. I mean, that's not what we…'

'I wouldn't worry about it.'

'I know *you* wouldn't worry about it but what if…?'

'I'm pretty sure he died quickly. See,' and Harris pointed to the large gash across the back of de Luca's skull. 'That would do for you pretty much instantaneously.'

'I hope you're right.' Crowther did not sound convinced.

'At least we found him,' said Harris.

They heard someone cursing behind them and turned to see Matty Gallagher picking his way awkwardly across the boulders, trying not to scuff his shoes. Harris and Crowther exchanged amused glances. Aged in his mid-thirties, more than a decade younger than Harris, the detective sergeant was an altogether different proposition from his colleague. Whereas Harris was tall and muscular, his face strong-jawed, the blue eyes piercing and his thick brown hair without a hint of grey, Gallagher was short and stocky and lacked the athleticism of his colleague. His black hair was starting to go bald, giving him the appearance of a monk. Showing the first signs of grey flecking, the sergeant had the look of a man starting to show his age, even more so this day because of the scowl on his face. London born-and-bred, the high hills were not his world; he felt uneasy in the wide-open spaces of the uplands. Matty Gallagher needed people: it was the reason he had tried, so far without success, to obtain a transfer to one of the constabulary's larger towns on the flatlands well to the east of Levton Bridge.

Now, having spent the morning complaining his way across the fell, Gallagher clambered with some difficulty over the last boulder, cursing as he barked his shin.

'Can't these people die in more convenient places?' he said, pausing to rub his leg and tutting as he saw the scratch marks on his shoes. 'Look at the state of them. Cost me ninety-five quid, they did.'

'Bloody townie,' grunted Harris. 'I told you to borrow a pair of my walking boots.'

Gallagher ignored the comment and pulled his blue windcheater tighter around him as a chill wind blew through the quarry.

'I assume it's de Luca?' he said, nodding at the body.

Harris nodded.

'That'll please you,' said the sergeant. 'One less on the planet.'

Harris allowed himself a slight smile but Bob Crowther said nothing: many years working alongside police officers had accustomed him to their banter. Besides, he knew that the sergeant's comment reflected the inspector's views pretty accurately. Everyone knew that Jack Harris had no time for those who preyed on wildlife. It was not as if he made a secret of it.

'So,' said Gallagher, glancing up at the cliff, 'do we assume he fell trying to get the eggs?'

'Not so sure,' said Harris.

'You reckon it's dodgy?'

'Bob reckons he might have been dragged here.'

'Could just be where he fell, though,' Gallagher pointed out, looking up to the top of the cliff. 'Doesn't look very secure.'

'Maybe,' said Crowther, glancing across the quarry then back up the cliff, 'but I'd have expected him to land a few feet further out. See that ledge that runs all the way round? Well, I reckon he would have hit that on his way down.'

'What's more,' said Harris, 'a fall doesn't fit with what Geordie Carroll said. He reckoned they were leaving the quarry. If he's right, how come chummy ended up back here?'

'*If* he's right,' said Gallagher.

'Why would he make a mistake like that?' asked Harris.

Gallagher saw Bob Crowther listening intently and did not reply. Noting the sergeant's discomfort, the rescue leader diplomatically walked a few feet away and stared across at his team, who were sitting by the dilapidated shed, drinking tea from flasks and chewing on sandwiches. None of them looked at the detectives: they had seen too many dead bodies to take much interest in the proceedings.

'Come on,' said Harris, looking at his sergeant, 'you've been itching to say it.'

'Ok,' said Gallagher in a low voice, 'Geordie has not exactly been forthcoming about where he went after he rang you, has he now? And I imagine you did not exactly give him the third degree.'

'Meaning?'

'You know what I mean, guv.'

Harris looked at him for a moment, torn, as ever, between loyalty to an old friend and his duty as a police officer. The police officer's instinct won out. It usually did and he knew that Gallagher was correct, that he had not pushed Carroll for an explanation when they spoke on the phone the previous evening.

'Maybe you're right,' said Harris grudgingly, then gestured at a figure picking its way effortlessly towards them. 'Talk of the devil.'

A tall and wiry man in his early fifties, with an angular face, thinning, grey hair and a wispy beard, Geordie Carroll was wearing brown cords and a green waterproof, the hood turned up against the rain. An experienced climber, he was wearing an orange helmet and had a length of rope slung over his shoulder, which he had used to abseil down the cliffside to check on the eagles' nest.

'Well?' shouted Harris. 'Did they get the eggs?'

Carroll nodded and Harris swore under his breath.

'I thought you lot had a 24-hour guard on the place,' said Gallagher, an edge in his voice as he looked at Carroll.

'These people are very clever,' said Carroll, nodding at the body. 'He dead then?'

Harris nodded.

'Good,' said Carroll. 'Any sign of the eggs?'

'No,' said Harris.

Carroll started to walk back across the quarry.

'I wonder if you would like to answer some questions before you go?' shouted Gallagher. 'Like...'

'Later,' said Carroll with a waft of the hand but not turning around. 'Ask me later.'

Watching him go, Gallagher frowned and glanced at the inspector, who was staring up at the eagles. The sergeant sighed, Harris might not hear alarm bells ringing out across the hills but he sure as hell did. Loud and clear.

'What do you want to do with the body?' asked Crowther, breaking into the sergeant's reverie.

'We're going to have to leave him here until we get everything sorted.' Harris glanced up at the darkening sky. 'Trouble is, this little lot looks like it's closing in.'

'Don't worry, we can sort some kind of shelter,' said Crowther, gesturing across to the dilapidated shed. 'Might find something useful in there.'

As he was speaking, Mike Ganton detached himself from the rescue team and headed towards them. As he neared, they could see that he was clutching a radio.

'I've just had Jim on,' said Ganton. 'I sent him and Archie to search the tops and they bumped into one of the shepherds. Billy Dent, works for old man Jessop over at Howgill Farm. He knows you, Hawk.'

'They all know Hawk,' murmured Gallagher.

'What did he tell you?' asked Harris, ignoring the comment.

'Reckons there was a stranger wandering across the fell yesterday, about the same time your guys were up here.'

'What does he mean, a stranger?'

'From the next village,' said Gallagher slyly, prompting a glare from the inspector. 'Different coloured cap.'

'He just said a stranger,' shrugged Ganton, giving the sergeant an odd look then glancing at Crowther. 'Hey, it's a long time since we've been here, Bob. Not since Jimmy Roscoe, in fact.'

'Who was Jimmy Roscoe?' asked Gallagher.

'Bloke who went missing fifteen years ago now,' said Ganton. 'Not long after the quarry closed. Never did find him.'

'What happened?'

'Went out one morning and never came back. Probably took a header down one of the mine shafts,' said Ganton, nodding out through the quarry entrance and onto the fells. 'There's dozens of them out there.'

'Yeah, they'd never find you,' said Crowther.

'Coming to think of it, he knew Paul de Luca, didn't he?' said Ganton, looking down at the body.

Harris nodded. 'They went to school together,' he said.

'They were both bad'uns,' said Crowther.

There was silence for a few moments then Crowther clapped Ganton on the shoulder.

'Come on, Mike,' he said. 'I've got a little job for you. Need you to move some ghosts out of that shed.'

Gallagher watched the two men walk across the quarry.

'What do you make of that?' he asked.

Harris did not reply.

'Oh, while I remember,' said Gallagher. 'The super has rung me three times. Says he can't get an answer out of your mobile.'

'You know what reception is like up here, Matty lad.'

'Aye, that'll be it,' said the sergeant. 'Apparently the lawyers for Rawmarsh and Hopson have arrived and are giving him a hard time.'

'I bet they are.'

Harris had known they would come. Of course he had. Indeed, because Rawmarsh was from Liverpool, the inspector had expected his solicitor to arrive the night before and was grateful when the lawyer said he was not prepared to risk travelling the moorland roads when they were shrouded with fog. Hopson's solicitor worked for a London firm and her PA had contacted the police station to confirm that she would not arrive until midday anyway. Harris resolved to put the confrontation off for a little while longer.

'You should get back to the office,' he said.

'Why?' asked the sergeant suspiciously.

'I'm needed out here.'

'And what do I tell Curtis?'

'Tell him whatever you want.'

'Do I tell him it's a murder?'

'It will make life very complicated if it is,' and the inspector gave the sergeant an exasperated look. 'I told Curtis but he wouldn't listen.'

'To be fair, you only warned him about some birds' eggs. I don't recall you saying anything about someone stoving Paul de Luca's head in.'

Harris looked as if he was about to remonstrate – to him, the loss of the eggs was as near to murder as you could get and certainly a much greater tragedy than the death of de Luca – but he thought better of it. He knew the sergeant would never understand. No one ever did.

'Look on the positive side, though,' continued Gallagher. 'You'll have to take yourself off shed break-ins after this.'

Harris allowed himself a slight smile.

'In fact,' said Gallagher, starting to walk across the quarry, 'I am beginning to wonder if you didn't push him yourself. See you later.'

'Don't fall down a mine shaft on your way back,' said Harris. 'You'd never get your transfer then.'

Gallagher paused in mid-stride, looked like he was about to say something but thought better of it and continued walking. Harris watched him go then glanced up again at the golden eagle, now huddled with its mate on a ledge half way up the cliffside. The inspector felt a sudden rush of anger as he recalled his joy when he heard about the nest and the dark despair that followed when he realised that the egg collectors had robbed it. He had never had children – his one marriage, when he was eighteen and serving with the Army in Germany, had been brief, stormy and without issue – but the sensations he experienced now were as if one of his own had been taken from him. Harris looked up at the brooding skies and struggled with an overwhelming sense that the equilibrium of his beloved hills had been disturbed. He did not quite understand it but it felt like violation, as if things were happening that were beyond his control and that they were somehow about him as well as Paul de Luca. That this was about more than the death of one man. Harris walked over to stare down at the lifeless body. As he did so, he heard the male eagle cry high above him, its voice high and fluted on the heavy air. The chief inspector leaned down until he was within inches of de Luca's face.

'I almost wish I had pushed you, you bastard,' he muttered. 'Should have done it years ago.'

The rain drove even harder, creating small pools beneath the corpse.

Chapter three

It was as the mountain rescue team carried de Luca's body across the fells that afternoon, the grey skies and driving rain creating a fittingly sombre atmosphere, that the inspector's mobile phone rang. Without breaking stride, he reached into his coat pocket but did not glance down to see the name on the screen. He guessed who it was. Harris had been ignoring calls from Superintendent Curtis for several hours. He wanted to let the commander sweat a little longer. Gallagher, who had rung several times since arriving back at the station, had already reported that the superintendent was increasingly unnerved by what was happening.

Harris knew what was worrying Curtis. The superintendent had made it clear when he took charge at Levton Bridge that he did not like Harris's penchant for taking on bird persecution cases when he should be concentrating on what Curtis called 'proper police work.' The commander's view was simple: the public wanted detectives to arrest burglars not people who attacked animals, so he constantly ignored the inspector's claims that wildlife criminals were involved in other kinds of offences as well.

Harris had always reckoned there was more to the superintendent's attitude than simply a difference in policing. The inspector had come to believe that the ever-ambitious Curtis resented the fact that involvement with wildlife crimes had made Jack Harris a nationally-known figure, often called on to give media interviews and to address high-profile national conferences, events at which the inspector made no secret of his disgust at the lack of support from the police service. Curtis had several times commented on the inspector taking time off to attend such events: apart from the presence of Scoot in the superintendent's station, the inspector's high profile was the biggest bone of contention between the commander and the detective. So, Harris knew that the moment Curtis heard that a murder was linked to an attack on the eagles, he would have immediately started worrying about the political implications.

Indeed, Curtis had, according to Gallagher, already visited the CID squad room several times that afternoon, each time appearing distracted and occasionally running a hand through what remained of his thinning hair as he demanded to know where the DCI was and complaining that the detective was not answering his phone. Harris, for his part, had found his enjoyment increasing every time he ignored the commander's name when it flashed up on his mobile phone screen. Expecting the same again this time, he finally glanced down and smiled broadly when he saw the word 'Leckie' appear instead. He took the call.

'Now then,' said Harris, continuing to walk briskly across the moorland path, his feet squelching on the damp earth and a muddy Scoot trotting at his heels. 'Wondered when you'd ring.'

'Heard that you've been having some fun and games,' said the voice on the other end. 'Any truth in the rumour that your victim is none other than our Mister de Luca?'

'The very same.'

'When's the party? Can I bring the balloons?'

Harris chuckled. He had always appreciated Graham Leckie's dark sense of humour. The uniformed constable was one of the inspector's closest friends in the police service. Few people at Levton Bridge – if any – had grown close to Jack Harris but that did not mean that he did not make friends elsewhere. Leckie was one of them. An officer in the Greater Manchester force, he had first met Harris at an RSPB conference more than a decade before, the two men sat next to each other as they avidly took notes during a seminar. They had instinctively connected through their passion for the subject and spent every spare moment of the event comparing notes.

Discovering that they both worked for Greater Manchester Police – Harris had just taken up his first posting as a police officer after leaving the Army – they met regularly to swap information about wildlife crime. Even when Harris moved north, they talked regularly on the phone and, Manchester being little over an hour and a half down the motorway from Levton Bridge, still met for a drink several times a year. Leckie's main job was in intelligence so, having heard the rumours that one of his local villains was dead, the constable had made some phone calls. Intrigued by what he had heard, he contacted his friend on Dead Hill.

'So, is it murder?' asked Leckie.

'Won't know until tomorrow,' said Harris, stopping mid-stride to glance behind him at the rescue team as they carefully carried their burden across the fell, 'but I'd put my last dollar on it being iffy. I'm holding Eddy Rawmarsh and Gerald Hopson.'

'What, all because of the eagle eggs?' Leckie's voice was incredulous.

'Yeah, why not?'

'Because egg collectors don't murder each other. Besides, the word down here is that there has been some kind of big falling out. De Luca did something to annoy our local villains. I'll ask around, find out a bit more.'

'You do that,' said Harris, staring thoughtfully at the body being carried past him, 'because that could just be what I call motive, Leckie boy.'

'Good spot,' said Leckie, 'that's why you're a DCI and I'm just some humble plod.'

The comment still had Jack Harris laughing as the procession turned off the fell and started to work its way through the bog.

The man crouched behind a boulder and surveyed from a distance the slow progress of Paul de Luca's body across the fells. He had been watching events unfold at the quarry for most of the day. It had been a testing time, requiring all his skills of concealment as he watched the comings and goings.

He was pretty confident that no one had seen him through the film of rain, although there had been an uneasy moment when Harris had glanced in his direction, pausing in mid-stride before continuing to tramp across the fells, dog at his heels. The man had felt a chill go through his body: he tried to convince himself that it was the result of hours exposed to the damp of the hills but he knew it was more than that. The last thing he wanted was a confrontation with Jack Harris. The thought of the detective's anger at the loss of the eggs was a disquieting prospect and the man resolved to abandon his surveillance and leave the hills in the other direction: there was a gully down which he could descend unseen. Few people even knew of its existence. No point in pushing his luck. He took a final look across the fells after the departing procession.

'Bye bye, Paul,' he said with a dry laugh and started to lope in the other direction.

On the drive back to Levton Bridge, Jack Harris decided to seek out Billy Dent, the shepherd who had reported seeing the stranger the day before. He knew where to find him and, not long after leaving the car park where the inspector had seen de Luca's body loaded into an ambulance, he swung his Land Rover off the road and up a winding track. Drawing to a halt half-way up, he got

out and surveyed Howgill Farm as it nestled in the lee of
Dead Hill, the lights in the house already gleaming in the
gathering gloom. Standing in silence, he looked to his
right, out across fields rapidly becoming shrouded in mist
as the rain started to fall again. Harris glanced up at the
brooding sky and gave a slight smile: he loved weather like
this. Sitting beside him, Scoot sniffed the gatepost then
looked up and gave a whimper. The detective glanced
down as the dog's ears pricked.

'What you seen?' he asked.

Peering into the mist, the inspector saw what he was
looking for, a lone figure striding down from the moor,
dog at heel.

'Bang on time,' said Harris, looking over to the
farmhouse again. 'Won't want to miss Edna Jessop's tea
and scones.'

The inspector watched Billy Dent make his way across
the fields for several minutes until he was close enough to
see him clearly. Dent was a wiry little man in his late
forties, dressed as ever in brown cords, mud-spattered
from his day on the hills, and a fustian jacket with ragged
cuffs. A flat cap was jammed onto his head. Seeing Harris
standing by the edge of the field, Dent raised a hand in
salutation.

'Now then, Jack,' he said as he neared. 'You after me?'

'Well I'm not waiting for a bus,' said Harris, shaking
the hand proffered by the shepherd and marvelling as ever
at the vice-like grip. 'Seems like you saw someone
interesting yesterday.'

Dent seemed, at first, to not have heard the comment.
Instead he glanced down and issued a sharp command to
his black and white collie, who settled down at the
shepherd's feet, pointedly ignoring Scoot.

'So, who did you see?' asked Harris.

'I told them lads it was nowt.'

'Maybe it is when I've got a man dead.'

'Aye, I heard your lot were up there,' said Dent, glancing up at the hill. 'Who were it, Jack? Anyone I know?'

'Paul de Luca.'

'Not sure anyone will miss him.'

'Indeed not. So, what did you see?'

'Just a man,' said Dent with a shrug. 'A hiker. Blue coat on. Heading off towards Hellens Wood.'

'Any idea who he was?'

Was it the chief inspector's imagination or did Billy Dent hesitate for a moment? Did a sense of unease flicker across his eyes? Jack Harris could not be sure and, if it had, the expression had gone in an instant.

'Too far away,' said Dent and made a clicking noise, at which his dog got to its feet. 'See you later, Jack, lad.'

Harris watched in silence as the shepherd strode towards the farmhouse, dog at his feet. The inspector turned back to stare across the hill as the rain fell even harder, sweeping across the fields in great sheets. For some reason, memories of Jimmy Roscoe danced before his eyes.

* * *

The rain had stopped and dusk was settling over Levton Bridge by the time a pensive Jack Harris returned to the police station. He parked his Land Rover at the front of the building, even though the superintendent had issued a memo in which he said staff vehicles should be left in the back yard. After exchanging a few words with the journalists and camera crews waiting on the other side of the road, attracted to the town by news of the death of Paul de Luca, Harris bounded up the front steps to the station, followed enthusiastically by Scoot.

At the top, the inspector hesitated, hand on door handle, as he peered through the glass into the cramped little reception area. Curtis, a tall, thin man with sharply angular features, was being harangued by a tubby man with a sallow, almost yellowing, complexion and lank black hair, a lock of which kept flopping over his eyes, forcing him to brush it away irritably. Dressed in a shabby black suit and with scuffed shoes, the man was in stark contrast to the other person in the reception, an elegant brunette in a smart grey coat who was standing slightly apart from the men as she listened intently to the argument with Curtis, occasionally nodding her head in agreement and gesticulating with long fingers.

Harris surveyed her for a moment or two. The usual word for someone that sophisticated in Levton Bridge was 'lost', he thought, as he looked at the beautifully-coiffured hair and the brown eyes, partially concealed by slightly tinted spectacles. Noticing her deep red lipstick, the inspector was reminded of a woman he had slept with during a few days' leave when his regiment was stationed in the Middle East. Images of her face drifted into his mind and the inspector struggled vainly to recall her name. Perhaps he never even knew it. More than likely.

Peering through the glass, he let his gaze range slowly down the woman's slim frame to the glimpse of shapely legs in dark stockings, and to her expensive black shoes. If Gallagher were here, thought Harris, he would presumably say that her footwear was Italian or something but then the inspector had never understood the sergeant's obsession with shoes. Harris tried to guess the woman's age: thirty-five, forty? No more. But then he had never been good at judging women's ages. He instinctively ran a hand through his damp, tousled hair in a vain attempt to make it look tidier. Realising what he had done, he chuckled.

'Down boy,' he said.

Scoot glanced up at his master.

'Not you,' said Harris.

Dragging his thoughts, with some difficulty, away from the woman and back to the scruffy man haranguing Curtis, Harris sighed: seventeen years in the job were more than enough for him to know lawyers when he saw them. And attractive or not, the fact that the woman was also clearly a solicitor immediately put him on his guard. For a few moments, the inspector contemplated walking back down the steps and leaving Curtis to handle the aggravation but it was too late because the divisional commander caught sight of him and gestured with his hand. Harris sighed again and pushed his way through the door, catching a hint of perfume as he did so. He had no idea what the scent was – he had never been into such things, not even when he was married – but it smelled expensive. The woman did not acknowledge his presence.

'I am sure Detective Chief Inspector Harris can answer your questions, Mr Hadleigh,' said the superintendent. 'And yours as well, Ms Reynolds. I would quite like to hear the answers myself.'

'Sorry, guv,' said Harris, patting his coat pocket. 'Dodgy reception up on the hills. You know how it is.'

'Indeed,' muttered Curtis.

The superintendent, having looked balefully down at Scoot, who was sniffing Hadleigh's leg with interest, made his excuses and disappeared through a side door. Harris watched him go gloomily then looked at the lawyers without much enthusiasm.

'And how can I help you?' he asked in a voice that suggested he did not care.

'I take it you are in charge of this investigation?' said Hadleigh, irritably flicking his foot to get rid of the dog.

'I am.'

'Then you have a lot of questions to answer,' said Hadleigh, wagging a pudgy finger at the detective chief inspector.

'And so have you,' said Harris calmly. 'Let's start with who the fuck you are, shall we?'

William Hadleigh seemed momentarily lost for words. The woman eyed him with the faintest of smiles then glanced back at the impassive detective, raising an eyebrow as she did so. It was almost as if she was enjoying the confrontation, thought Harris. The inspector found himself intrigued by the woman's reaction. Lawyers normally jumped up and down on their soapbox when he said such things but the woman seemed unruffled by his aggressive approach. The inspector waited for the stuttering Hadleigh to regain his composure.

'I,' said the lawyer at last, trying to appear dignified, but failing dismally, 'am William Hadleigh, of Hadleigh, Coyne and Reckitt.'

Harris shrugged.

'If you talk to your colleagues in Liverpool,' said Haleigh, 'they will tell you that I am well known in the city.'

'What did they nick you for?'

A smile twitched on the woman's lips.

'I hardly think this is time for flippant remarks,' snapped Hadleigh. 'I am Eddy Rawmarsh's lawyer and you have kept him in a cell for an entire day without good reason. I did not come all this way to be left hanging around in this disgraceful fashion.'

'It's hardly an epic journey,' said Harris, glancing down the steps at the silver Jaguar parked next to his Land Rover.

'I, on the other hand,' said Ella Reynolds, 'have endured a somewhat longer, and distinctly more unpleasant, journey from London, the final stages of it spent sitting next to a scruffy man who appeared to have little sense of personal hygiene.'

'Oh, you came up together did you?' said Harris blandly.

Hadleigh glowered at him.

'I came on the train,' said Reynolds coldly. 'And I arrived to find that you have disappeared, that no one is prepared to give me a straight answer about my client, who might I add is increasingly distressed by this whole experience, and that your Superintendent Curtis seems incapable of speaking anything even remotely approaching common sense.'

'At least that's something we can agree on,' murmured Harris.

'So,' continued Reynolds, fixing the detective with a keen look, 'I really think you do owe us an explanation. And I would like to resolve this quickly and get back to London tonight, if at all possible.'

'Well, that won't happen,' said Harris, holding open a side door to an interview room. 'Shall we?'

Having turned to utter a command to Scoot, who obediently lay down in a corner of the reception area, Harris followed the solicitors into the room and smiled disarmingly. Without the post mortem results, he did not even know for definite if he was looking at a murder so the inspector sensed that the time had come to calm things down, particularly as Gallagher said that Hadleigh had been making a series of shrill threats about wrongful arrest. Harris, aware that the suggestion had unnerved Curtis, and acutely conscious that his standing with the divisional commander was not high, resolved to avoid confrontation as best he could. He took a seat at the table.

'The reason your clients were held overnight,' he began, choosing his words carefully, 'is that they were both with Paul de Luca before his death yesterday.'

'But like we repeatedly told your superintendent,' said Reynolds, 'there is no evidence to substantiate that claim. My client believes your witness was mistaken. A genuine, and perhaps understandable, mistake but a mistake all the same. I understand Mr Rawmarsh is of the same opinion.'

'Come on,' protested Harris. 'Eddy Rawmarsh could lie for England.'

Hadleigh opened his mouth to retort but a look from Reynolds strangled any words in his throat.

'That remains to be seen,' she said, 'but I can assure you that Mr Hopson is a man not given to lying. May I ask what you plan to do with him?'

'I would like both of them to stay in Levton Bridge tonight.'

'I have heard of northern hospitality but is that not a touch excessive?'

'There are several lines of inquiry that we are pursuing.'

'Then you should put them to our clients,' said Reynolds. 'I understand you have been somewhat vague in your dealings with them.'

'I need more time.'

'Might I suggest that you have run out of time, Chief Inspector? Unless my client is a formal suspect, I do not really think you can keep him any longer. Might bail solve your dilemma?'

'And just how long do you think it would be before Hopson scuttled off home? No offence, Ms Reynolds, but I don't fancy going to London to bring him back. It's not my favourite place in the world.'

Ella Reynolds looked at the inspector, his hair still damp from his long hours on the fells and his face flecked with mud.

'No, I imagine it isn't,' she said. 'Look, Chief Inspector, I am prepared to cut you a deal. You let my client go and I will ensure he presents himself for interview tomorrow morning. I am sure Mr Hadleigh will give you the same undertaking.'

Harris considered the offer: the thought of Eddy Rawmarsh walking free from the police station caused him more than a little unease. However, the inspector also realised that, given the paucity of hard facts, bail was his only option. And for some reason he could not quite explain, he trusted Ella Reynolds.

'Ok,' he nodded and looked hard at Hadleigh. 'But I expect Eddy to turn up as well. No tricks, do you hear?'

'He'll be there,' said Hadleigh, 'and I would hope that your attitude towards me in the morning is a distinct improvement on…'

'Well, that's it, I think,' said Ella Reynolds, cutting across him, standing up and reaching for her briefcase.

Hadleigh gaped at her, mouth opening and shutting, rather, thought Harris, like a scruffy goldfish.

'And since it would appear that I will not be travelling back to London tonight after all,' said Reynolds, 'I need somewhere to stay. Any suggestions, Chief Inspector?'

'There's a nice little guest house just off the market place,' said Harris. 'Well, I say nice, at least it's got carpets where you can still see the colour.'

'I suppose it is asking too much that Levton Bridge has a decent wine bar?'

Harris thought of the smoky spit-and-sawdust pubs clustered round the market place and images flashed into his mind of beer-swilling farmhands and drunken women in short skirts and poorly-applied slap. Images of raucous laughter and brawls spilling out into the street.

'You know,' he said, 'I think it probably is, Ms Reynolds.'

Chapter four

It was as Jack Harris was crossing the market place that evening, having purchased a sandwich at the corner shop, that the man approached him. The inspector smiled a welcome: he had known Barry Ramsden for many years and had voted for the optician when the poll was held for the parish council.

'Can I have a word?' said Ramsden.

'Sure,' said Harris as they started walking towards the police station. 'What about?'

'Those men you arrested for murdering Paul de Luca. The word is you have released them.'

'And how would you know that?' asked the inspector, turning and looking at his friend, the smile fading.

'They have just booked a couple of rooms at the King's Head.'

'My, word does travel fast,' said Harris, negotiating his way down the small flight of steps past the councillor's opticians shop.

'You know this place.'

'Only too well, Barry.'

'Look,' said Ramsden, stopping, 'this is rather awkward but we were rather hoping that you would have charged them by now.'

Harris surveyed Ramsden for a few moments, noting that the parish chairman was perspiring slightly.

'At this moment,' said the inspector, 'I do not even know if there is anything to charge anyone with. For all I know, Paul de Luca fell.'

'But if there had been anything untoward,' insisted Ramsden, 'you would charge them, yes?'

Harris looked at him sharply.

'What's this about, Barry?'

'The b. & b. people are talking. The last thing they want is folks getting the idea that there is a killer running round the hills. It's bad for business.'

'How're Jenny Hargreaves' corneas?'

'What?'

'You know, Jenny Hargeaves. She said she was coming to see you – her sight is a bit misty, she says. Particularly the right eye. I wonder what you prescribed.'

'What the hell has that got to do with anything?' asked the councillor.

'Just thought I'd tell you how to do your job,' said Harris and walked briskly round the corner.

Once he was out of sight, he allowed himself the broadest of grins. Half an hour later, he was sitting in his office, the remnants of his sandwich on the desk in front of him. He shook his head as he ran through the conversation in his mind and waited for the kettle on the windowsill to boil. Scoot was curled up under the desk, asleep after his long walk across the hills earlier in the day. Harris stared moodily out of the window, looking across the market place and onto the gathering darkness of late afternoon on the fells beyond the town. Flecks of rain had begun to rattle off the glass once more – it had been a wet spring – and the inspector's thoughts were transported back to the quarry. Its peace would have been restored again by now, the forensics team long since gone. The quarry would once more be the domain of the golden eagles, and their cold and empty nest. Harris pursed his lips at the idea and, without realising it, clenched his right hand. Noticing what he had done, he straightened out his fingers and took several deep breaths. Anger management, Jack, anger management, he told himself.

His reverie was interrupted by a light knock on the door – in walked Matty Gallagher.

'Any news?' asked Harris, standing up and walking over to the windowsill as the kettle started to wheeze.

'We've finally tracked down de Luca's brother. You were right – he lives in Manchester. Had a brief chat with him on his mobile.'

'And is Robert on his way up here?'

'He's coming back from business abroad, due back late tonight. Says he'll be here tomorrow. Says he knows you.'

'Did he seem upset?'

'About knowing you?' said the sergeant with a sly look. 'Not unduly.'

'I meant about his brother,' said Harris, allowing himself a smile: there were times when Gallagher's humour proved an effective antidote to the darker side of the job. 'Did he seem upset that Paul was dead?'

'Not really. I got the impression that they were not particularly close.'

'They haven't been for a long time,' said Harris.

'So how do you know th…?'

'What's that?' asked Harris, gesturing to a sheaf of papers in the sergeant's hand.

The sergeant frowned: he had still not got used to the inspector's direct ways.

'It's Paul de Luca's record,' said Gallagher, dropping the papers onto the desk. 'Assault, burglary, handling, auto crime, a couple of assaults. Not exactly Mother Teresa, was he?'

'Not exactly,' said Harris, glancing at the other papers still in the sergeant's hand. 'So, what are *they*?'

'Stuff on that missing bloke that Mike Ganton mentioned. Jimmy Roscoe.'

'For why?'

'Just seemed a strange coincidence that they came to a bad end in the same place. And Mike Ganton seemed to suggest that they knew each other, so I thought I would dig a bit deeper.'

'Can't really see the point,' said Harris, reaching down to test the warmth of the kettle. 'We've got more pressing things to worry about.'

'With all due respect…'

'Not another one going to tell me how to do my job?' said Harris waspishly.

'What does that mean?'

'Barry Ramsden cornered me outside demanding to know why I had not had Rawmarsh and Hopson hung, drawn and quartered. Apparently the natives are getting restless.'

'Why?'

'Long story. Ok, convince me that Jimmy Roscoe has got something to do with this.'

'Call it a copper's instinct. Mike Ganton was spot on. 1993. Jimmy set off one morning to walk across the hills…'

'He loved doing that, did our Jimmy.'

'You knew *him* as well?'

'As I keep telling you, everyone knows everyone up here. If you really want to know, I went to school with Jimmy Roscoe.'

'You did?'

'Levton Bridge Primary.' Harris gave a slight smile. 'He was the one who first called me Hawk.'

'Why did you not mention this before?' Gallagher's voice had a slightly accusing tone to it.

It was not lost on Harris.

'Because,' said the inspector curtly, 'I really can't see the relevance. It was a long time ago and has no bearing whatsoever on what has happened to Paul de Luca. All the evidence pointed to him having some kind of accident. There was nothing to put de Luca or anyone else there with him when it happened.'

'But before Jimmy came home, he was in Liverpool. And that is Eddy Rawmarsh's neck of the woods, guv.'

'You're fishing, Matty lad,' said the inspector, reaching for a mug as the kettle came to the boil.

'Maybe not,' said the sergeant earnestly. 'Look, we know that Eddy Rawmarsh has a record for car crime and you know what Jimmy was doing in Liverpool, I take it?'

'Nicking cars.'

'Bit more than that, guv. He and his brother were running a chop-shop. That's where they cut up cars and…'

'I know what a chop shop is.'

'Sorry, I just thought…'

'Yeah, I know what you thought,' snapped the inspector, turning round quickly, kettle in hand. 'I've told you before, just because you worked in the Met doesn't make you some kind of sodding hot-shot.'

'Sorry,' said Gallagher, inwardly cursing himself for the lapse.

The inspector nodded and returned to pouring the water.

'Want one?' he asked.

'No thanks. Anyway,' said Gallagher, trying to sound more respectful, 'this is where the story gets interesting, or at least I think it does. Merseyside Police raided the brothers' workshop one night. Garry Roscoe gets a year, Jimmy gets eight months, out in five, after which he comes back home to his old mum.'

'She still lives in Chapel Ebton,' nodded Harris.

'Anyway, Jimmy had not been back for that long when he disappeared. I just want to make sure there are no links. I mean, he did know de Luca.'

'Still can't see it. There was never anything to suggest that Paul de Luca was involved with the Roscoes on their car scam.'

'Why are you so against this?' said the sergeant, unable to hide his exasperation. 'Ok, so maybe I am wasting my time, at least I'm doing something.'

'Meaning?' said the inspector sharply.

'Nothing.'

'No, go on. Say it.'

Gallagher eyed the inspector dubiously; it was not the first time they had clashed over policing methods and the last thing he wanted was to damage even further what was already a fragile relationship.

'I just think,' he said, choosing his words carefully, 'that we should be doing more, maybe asking a few more questions about de Luca, putting feelers out, instead of sitting here doing sod all.'

'Actually, I *have* been asking some questions but, as it stands, we do not even know if Paul de Luca was murdered and until we do, there is not much else we can do. And digging up some story from the past will not help us.'

'Yes, but...'

'Look, I know you mean well,' said Harris, his voice softening as he noticed the sergeant's crestfallen expression, 'but this is a very closed community. It's different from the city. They're already worried enough about de Luca's death and if you suddenly start asking questions about Jimmy Roscoe as well, particularly without good reason, all it will do is re-open old wounds.'

'Ok, point taken,' nodded Gallagher, dragging up a chair and encouraged by the inspector's lightening of mood. 'But humour me anyway, will you? Tell me about Jimmy's disappearance. I am right, he was last seen near the quarry?'

'Yeah, it's not far from Ebton Chapel if you go over the tops,' said Harris – the inspector had done the walk many times with Scoot. 'Mind, it wasn't much of a sighting, just some hiker.'

'And no one reported seeing Jimmy after that?'

'Not as far as I know. Mind, I wasn't working here at the time.'

'People seem to reckon Jimmy fell down one of the old mine shafts,' said Gallagher. 'What do you think?'

'There were plenty of wild rumours at the time but I reckon that's the best bet. There's certainly plenty of them. I nearly lost Scoot down one a couple of years back. Didn't I, boy?' Harris smiled as the dog looked up and gave a little yip. 'You could search for years and never find Jimmy Roscoe, poor bastard.'

'Not sure anyone took that much interest, guv.'

'Meaning?'

'Meaning,' said Gallagher, lowering his voice even though the office door was closed, 'that it was a piss-poor investigation.'

Harris considered the sergeant's comments. Although he was renowned for defending friends and colleagues from criticism, he had to admit that there had always been something about the case that had worried him. Something that did not quite fit. Once more, as he sat there, memories came flooding back, days in the schoolyard, rough and tumble games of football, fun-fights with their cut knees and bust lips, and of Jimmy Roscoe with his perpetually beaming face. Why had Harris done nothing about his concerns until now, he asked himself. Why had he not sought to re-open the inquiry when he assumed command of divisional CID? Old wounds or not, it was surely his duty to consider doing so, but what had stopped him? He could hardly blame overwork. Not up here. Laziness, perhaps? Complacency, more like, he thought. Or maybe a reluctance to disturb the routine of an existence spent working his hours and walking the dog. This place did that to you, thought Harris. He knew that only too well. He'd seen it in other officers as well.

Noticing Gallagher eying him intently, the inspector nodded: there was no point in further disillusioning a good sergeant who had already made no secret of wishing to leave Levton Bridge.

'Maybe you should take another look if you feel that strongly about it,' said Harris.

'Thank you,' said the sergeant and he meant it. 'I'll do it quietly.'

'You do that,' said Harris then glanced up at the clock on the wall. 'But do it tomorrow. Haven't you got a date with the fragrant Julie?'

'Shit, I nearly forgot,' exclaimed Gallagher.

Julie Marr was the reason Gallagher had moved to Levton Bridge five months previously. He met the bubbly blonde when both of them were working in London. Gallagher was a detective constable at the time, Julie a nurse. She had been born in Levton Bridge and her parents still lived in the area so, eventually, the pull of the north proved too strong and she announced to a horrified Gallagher that she wanted to go home. For Gallagher, it presented him with the toughest decision of his life, but with heavy heart, and after deliberating for several days, he put his love for Julie before his love for the bright lights of the capital and, with heavy heart, applied for a transfer, securing a posting to Levton Bridge.

Shortly after their move north, the couple had married. For a few weeks, they had lived close to Julie's parents, but, finding life in Levton Bridge too claustrophobic, had moved an hour's drive down the valley to Roxham, where Julie worked at the hospital. Although only a small market town, Roxham was larger than Levton Bridge and did at least have a smattering of restaurants and wine bars. Another attraction was that the west coast railway line allowed Matty to get to London in a few hours if he wished to see his family or hook up with friends. Julie never demurred when he took off; she realised that drinking sessions in old haunts were his way of coping with what he saw as the stifling nature of life in the hills.

Jack Harris was not insensitive to Gallagher's needs either and had noted that the sergeant had been talking about the couple's planned night out for days, ever since he discovered that Julie had a night off. Indeed, he had talked so much about it that Harris had written the event in his diary in large red letters. Jack Harris was certainly not about to make the mistake of overlooking something that important.

'Where are you taking her again?' asked the inspector, trying to sound interested.

'That new Italian place down on the bridge. La Sorrentina. Very nice, apparently. Reminds me of when we were in London, there was this really nice place we used to go to in the West End. Very nice food.' The sergeant's eyes adopted a far-away expression. 'Very nice indeed.'

'Yeah, I've heard of that kind of thing. Something called pizza, I think? Cheese and tomato cooked on a piece of bread with olives and all kinds of things on it,' said Harris, a hint of wonder in his voice. 'Sounds a bit exotic to me, mind.'

Gallagher looked at him in bemusement then Harris threw back his head and roared with laughter. As always when the inspector laughed, it caught Gallagher by surprise. It was the first time he had seen him do it in days and, as ever when it happened, the sergeant could never work out if it was a good sign or a bad sign. He decided not to even try. It was, he had long since decided, a waste of time trying to read the moods of Jack Harris.

'Go on,' grinned Harris, gesturing to the office door. 'Have a pleasant evening and give my love to Julie.'

'Thanks,' said Gallagher. 'You got any plans?'

Harris did not reply: they both knew the answer.

* * *

That evening, as rain lashed Dead Hill, Jack Harris sat alone in his living room, head buried in a book.

Occasionally, he would stare over his reading glasses into the crackling flames of the coal fire and mull over the events of the day. Home for Jack Harris was a tumbledown cottage on a narrow track halfway up one of the neighbouring slopes to Dead Hill, on the other side from Howgill Farm. That was why he had bought it. No people. Obscured from the winding road below by a fold in the hillside, the cottage stood in the shadow of a copse, whose conifers were now swaying and creaking as the winds battered the slopes. Harris had purchased the house after stumbling across the building while out on a walk with Scoot three years previously. At the time, the former shepherd's cottage had been in a dilapidated condition and the inspector was able to buy it at a knockdown price. It had taken him the best part of year to restore it to habitable condition, doing most of the tasks himself, working every spare hour he could, and calling in a few favours for the rest.

Now, he sat in the small, sparsely furnished living room, reclining comfortably in an old armchair, his feet propped up on a small wooden stool, Scoot curled up in front of the crackling fire, his body heaving rhythmically as he slumbered. From time to time, the inspector would reach down to ruffle his hair and Scoot would emit a small snuffling sound, but did not appear to wake. Harris was drinking whisky, his glass resting on a side table as he continued to read his book. As ever, it was about wildlife, the only thing he ever read apart from the odd thriller borrowed from the mobile library that visited Levton Bridge.

Although the antique bookcase in the corner of the room was piled high with books, many on the brink of toppling off the shelves, Jack Harris had come relatively late in life to reading but his time in the Army had changed everything. Finding himself, to his surprise, relishing the educational side of life in uniform, he had started to devour books as he sought something to fill the long hours between operations. Books were also a lifesaver when he came back to live in the valley, occupying his evenings during the long winter months when night came early and the wild gales howled and shrieked outside.

Books were less important to the chief inspector in summer when, after work, he and Scoot would invariably go on long walks, not returning until long after dusk had fallen, their tread sure and steady in the half-light of late evening. Although Harris enjoyed the occasions immensely, he did sometimes curse at the number of walkers still out on the hills at that time of night. That was why he much preferred winter. People thought him perverse but the reason was simple: the loneliness of the deserted hills connected with something deep inside his psyche.

Now, as he turned the page then reached for his glass, he tensed, arm half outstretched. Something had disturbed him. A noise half-heard in the haze of his third whisky? Or something imagined? He could not be sure so he sat motionless and listened for the best part of a minute but the noise did not come again. His thoughts went back to the movement he fancied he had seen on the ridge just before confronting Rawmarsh and Hopson the day before, and to the shadowy shape he thought he had glimpsed through the rain that afternoon as he accompanied de Luca's body down the hill. Harris frowned for a moment then looked down at Scoot, who was still peacefully asleep.

'Pull yourself together,' murmured the inspector and shook his head – he should know by now that the night played its own tricks.

Scoot looked up at the sound of his master's voice and fixed Harris with a quizzical look.

'Cheers, boy,' said the detective, mulling the whisky round for a few moments, appreciating the way the drink glinted in the firelight. 'Cheers.'

Scoot closed his eyes again.

As deepest night settled over the northern hills, the young moon largely obscured from sight by thick cloud cover, a lone figure picked its way along one of the country lanes outside Levton Bridge, the flickering light of his torch illuminating the way, the raindrops flickering in its beam. From time to time, he would hesitate and listen intently but he heard nothing except the pattering of the rain, the rustling of the trees and the occasional bleat of a sheep on a distant fell. After walking for a few more minutes, the man halted on a rise in the road and turned to survey the ornate metal gates to his right, set in a tall wire security fence. Levton Bridge Rare Breeds Centre, it said. Proprietor: R Corbett. The man glanced back down the slope towards Levton Bridge but nothing moved on its streets and although one or two houses had upstairs lights on, most of them were in darkness. The town was asleep. The night was his.

As the man stood surveying the slumbering town, he was startled by the screech of a tawny owl hunting in one of the nearby copses, followed by the scream of a vole as the bird's talons bit into its spine. Then there was silence. Rapidly regaining his composure – the sound had only momentarily alarmed him – the man gave a laugh. He waited for a few moments then returned his attention to the fence, slipped the backpack off his shoulder and produced a pair of wire-cutters. When, twenty minutes later, he slipped back out onto the road, rain had started to sweep across the hills.

Chapter five

'Where's the DCI?' demanded Ralph Corbett, looking expectantly at the young detective constable. 'I only talk to him.'

'I am afraid…' began Alison Butterfield.

'Get him on the radio. Tell him it's Ralph. Don't turn your nose up like that, young lady, just do it.'

Butterfield sighed. It was shortly after nine the following morning, the sky leaden and the air damp and heavy after the previous night's rain and they were standing at the heart of the smallholding that Corbett had run near Levton Bridge for more than ten years. Butterfield had never met him – she had always tried to avoid it, everyone knew what he was like – but she had heard Harris talk about him and knew that he was ex-job. Butterfield seemed to recall that he had transferred to Levton Bridge late in his career. From Merseyside, if her memory was right. She vaguely remembered Harris saying something about Corbett having to retire early because of a knee injury sustained as he tried to apprehend a burglar. Certainly, he had walked with a pronounced limp when he opened the front gate.

Now, they were standing amid a range of small enclosures containing a selection of bored-looking pigs, several scrawny goats and a couple of somewhat bedraggled donkeys that looked like they had seen better days. Butterfield knew that Corbett charged a small fee for tourists to visit what the sign at the entrance proclaimed to be a rare breeds centre, using the money as a way of eking out his police pension. God knows why anyone would visit this dump, she thought bleakly, surveying the rundown buildings and wrinkling her nose at the musty smell of neglect. Turning around, she spotted a small row of wooden cages along one wall, containing a selection of equally miserable-looking birds of prey. The detective constable did not care what type of birds they were: such matters were of little interest to her.

She looked back at Corbett, who was still making his demands, his arms crossed. *What was it about northern men that made them so belligerent when it came to women?* she asked herself. Butterfield had lost count of the times men had refused to talk to her during her inquiries in her three years in the job, the last eight months of her time spent at Levton Bridge. It seemed that Ralph Corbett was the same, which surprised her: after all, he was an ex-copper, surely he of all people should know how these things worked? She recalled Harris hinting that Corbett did not like women being police officers. From Corbett's expression, it seemed that the inspector was right.

Butterfield eyed him dubiously as he continued to talk at her. Aged in his early sixties, he was a jowly man with balding black hair, several strands of which were combed somewhat hopefully across his balding pate. He was wearing dirt-spattered blue overalls, which did little to contain his spreading stomach, and clutched a shovel in his hand. Corbett had, she surmised, been mucking out one of the enclosures when she arrived; not, she assumed from their grubby condition, something that he did often enough.

'Look, Mr Corbett,' she said, trying again to placate him. 'You are not…'

'I want to see the DCI and that's final. Hawk understands these things.'

Butterfield was about to reply when a harsh cry from one of the bird cages startled her.

'It's warning you off,' said Corbett and grinned, showing crooked front teeth. 'It doesn't like you.'

Butterfield shrugged. As the daughter of a local farmer, she had been brought up to regard all such creatures with suspicion. Indeed, when the eagles started to nest at the quarry, her father had muttered darkly about them taking his lambs. Not that she listened: since the arguments that followed her decision to give up a course at agricultural college and become a police officer instead, she and her father had spoken little. Before they stopped speaking, his dreams of her inheriting the farm in ruins because his other daughter was a trainee accountant, her father had argued that the slight blonde was too feeble to become a police officer. He kept coming back to his favourite scenario: that of his daughter confronting a burly burglar down a back alley at dead of night. When she told her father about the first time she arrested a housebreaker in such circumstances, enthusiastically recounting how she had twisted his arm behind his back and escorted the squealing man to the waiting police car, her father had walked wordlessly out of the room.

'Do you know what it is?' asked Corbett, nodding at the bird.

Butterfield shrugged.

'It's a Harris Hawk,' announced Corbett gleefully as Butterfield rolled her eyes skywards. 'So where *is* he?'

'DCI Harris is otherwise engaged, Mr Corbett. The job over at Dead Hill.'

'Yeah, I heard about it on the radio,' nodded Corbett, calming down slightly. 'That de Luca bloke. Don't reckon anyone will miss him.'

'What makes you say that?'

'They're scumbags, the lot of them, nicking them eggs. If you ask me, they should string…'

'Look,' said Butterfield in exasperation, 'can we stick to the matter in hand? You said on the phone that you'd had your shed done over.'

Corbett nodded and led her down a side path, past a series of tired enclosures containing pigs, to a ramshackle wooden building wedged into the furthest corner of the complex, standing between the fence and a tree whose boughs scraped the mossy roof. The shed door was hanging off its hinges and a quick glance inside revealed tools strewn across the floor.

'Anything stolen?' asked Butterfield, trying not to sound too bored: she had been feeling this way ever since Harris announced that he and Gallagher would handle the de Luca case.

'There's no need to sound like that. We can't all deal with dodgy deaths.'

'Who told you it was dodgy?' asked the constable.

'I just assumed so because it said on the radio that you had arrested two men. Anyway, forget that, this break-in is important to me, my girl, and when I was in the job, I always told my officers to treat all crimes the same. In fact, if I was still serving I might have been your boss. I finished up here, you know. In fact…'

'Yes, well you're not my boss. So, *has* anything been taken?'

Corbett shook his head, irked by her brusque tone.

'Nothing at all?' asked the detective constable. 'I mean, some of those tools look quite new. That saw has hardly been used. How come they didn't take that?'

'You're the copper,' said Corbett sulkily.

'There have been other break-ins and we reckon they're selling them at car boot sales. But this time,' she nodded at the shed, 'they left them. I just want to know why.'

Corbett said nothing.

'How did they get in?' asked Butterfield.

'Cut a hole in the fence. And how nice of you to ask.'

'Look,' said Butterfield, trying strike a more placatory tone: the last thing she wanted was another complaint to Superintendent Curtis about her attitude, 'I know these things are upsetting…'

'You have no idea.'

Corbett turned away to stare into one of the enclosures. Butterfield surveyed him with renewed interest. There was something in his demeanour that had alerted her instincts, a sense of things unsaid.

'This isn't just a shed burglary, is it?' she asked.

He stared at the ground, apparently fascinated by a weed poking through a crack in the path. Ignoring her comment, he crouched down and pulled the plant out before standing up and twisting it thoughtfully between his fingers.

'Mr Corbett,' said the detective constable, more insistent this time, 'is there something you want to tell me?'

'I'd rather talk to Hawk.'

'Well, he's not here.'

The edge in her voice made him look up. Eying her determined expression, he straightened up.

'This is not the first break-in here,' he said. 'Someone got in three weeks ago. And they came back the week after.'

'What did they take?'

'I don't think that's the point,' said Corbett, starting to walk down the path. 'Come with me. I've got something to show you.'

He led the way to a cabin close to the entrance. Inside it was an office.

'That was when I was a copper in Liverpool,' said Corbett, noticing her surveying the framed photograph of a pig on the wall, and managing a smile. 'One my sows had won best of breed in a show. You can imagine all the jokes the local rag put in the piece.'

Butterfield smiled as well: the quip seemed to have relaxed Corbett slightly. However, it was but a momentary relief and his face clouded over again as he reached into the top drawer of the desk to produce a photograph.

'That was the first break-in,' he said, handing it over.

Butterfield glanced at the image of red paint daubed along one side on the cabin, including a scrawled expletive clearly aimed at Corbett.

'Took me ages to scrub it off,' said Corbett and reached into the drawer to produce a second photograph, showing two of the cabin windows smashed. 'That was the other one.'

'Probably kids messing about. Besides, this new one feels different. I mean, there *have* been a lot of shed burglaries. Coming to think of it, we bailed someone before the de Luca thing blew up. He's desperate enough to go straight back on the rob. Needs it to pay for his smack. Maybe he got in but something scared him off.'

'Maybe,' but Corbett did not sound convinced.

Butterfield was surprised to see a new expression on his face. *What was it?* she wondered. Unease? Concern? No, stronger than that. Behind the obstinate front that he presented, Ralph Corbett was frightened. The realisation hit the detective constable with a jolt and she felt the hairs rising on the back of her neck.

'This isn't just kids, is it?' she asked.

Corbett considered the comment for a few moments.

'I think there's something you should know,' he said. 'You see, I can't help wondering if there's a link with the death of Paul de Luca.'

* * *

'Come on, Eddy,' snapped Harris. 'We know you were with de Luca the day he died.'

'And I say prove it,' replied Rawmarsh, sitting back in his seat and crossing his arms: he had been in too many police interview rooms to be fazed by the experience.

It was shortly after 10am and Harris and Gallagher had been questioning Rawmarsh for twenty minutes. The conversation had been given an extra edge by news that the pathologist at Roxham Hospital had confirmed that de Luca had a number of injuries and the one that killed him was a blow to the head. He said the most likely scenario was that he had been assaulted, although he could not entirely rule out a fall. On hearing the news from Harris, Eddy Rawmarsh had shown little emotion and the ensuing conversation had gone round in circles, the detectives finding new ways to phrase the same question, their suspect continually giving the same answer. At times, it seemed to the officers that he was enjoying himself, revelling in the chief inspector's growing frustration.

William Hadleigh was not so calm and his antics increasingly irritated Harris, as the solicitor fidgeted endlessly in his seat and continually interrupted proceedings. Each time Hadleigh intervened, the inspector's irritation became more apparent. Gallagher, noticing his colleague's bunched fist beneath the table, glanced at Harris several times, unable to conceal his concern: the sergeant had been here before.

'Might I suggest,' he said, 'that we try to calm down.'

'Look,' interrupted the inspector through gritted teeth, 'if he doesn't have anything to do with the death of Paul de Luca, why not at least admit to stealing the bloody eggs?'

'Because I have already said I do not know what you are on about,' said Rawmarsh.

'Yeah,' said Hadleigh belligerently. 'Perhaps you have a hearing problem, Chief Inspector. Perhaps you should buy yourself a…'

'Will you sodding well shut up!' snarled Harris, half-rising from the chair as his temper finally snapped.

Matty Gallagher moved swiftly to place a restraining hand on the detective inspector's arm. Harris glared at him but after seeing the warning look in the sergeant's eyes, gave a cursory nod and sat back down again, satisfying himself with glowering over the table at the smirking Rawmarsh and his startled solicitor.

'Hardly the actions we would expect from a police officer of your standing,' said Rawmarsh coolly.

'Well, what do you expect?' grunted Harris.

'Perhaps we should lodge a formal complaint for oppressive questioning. What do you think, Hadleigh?'

The lawyer nodded but continued to eye the inspector warily. Gallagher looked at Rawmarsh. Although the inspector's outburst had clearly alarmed the solicitor – Hadleigh had flinched when Harris leapt to his feet – it seemed to have had the opposite effect on Eddy Rawmarsh. Gallagher sensed that the inspector's furious reaction was exactly what he had been looking for. Everyone knew Jack Harris had a short fuse. It was rapidly becoming clear to Gallagher that the officers would have to afford Rawmarsh much more respect.

'I think cool heads are needed here,' said the sergeant, glancing at the inspector. 'From all of us.'

Harris said nothing.

'And you can wipe that smile off your face, Eddy,' said Gallagher. 'You are up to your neck in this one and we really are getting nowhere.'

'That's because there's nowhere to go. Your man fell off a cliff, that's all there is to it.'

'The pathologist's report would seem to suggest that he may have been assaulted. Besides, there's the fact that you were in the quarry with him. As was Hopson.'

'Prove it,' said Rawmarsh, sitting back and crossing his arms.

'Happy to,' said Gallagher, glancing down at the statement given by Geordie Carroll: it was time to crank up the pressure. 'You see, our witness has signed a statement that he saw you and Gerald Hopson at the quarry with de Luca. I suspect it is the kind of thing that a jury would find very convincing.'

'Is that all you've got?' said Rawmarsh, rapidly recovering his composure. 'Some nutter thinks he saw us? You are going to have to do better than that.'

'And de Luca's car was parked next to yours.'

'Yes, but it was not there when we arrived.'

'But when we put all this together with your little feud, it gets rather interesting.'

Rawmarsh started.

'Feud?' he said, but his voice sounded slightly strained. 'You're talking rubbish.'

'On the contrary: it seems that you had a falling-out with our friend Mr de Luca,' said the sergeant. 'In the eyes of a suspicious person like me, that looks rather like a motive unless there is an innocent explanation. Of course, if you continue to play games…'

The sergeant left the sentence unfinished. Rawmarsh murmured something to Hadleigh, who shook his head vigorously. They had a whispered conversation for the best part of a minute, the solicitor protesting, and glancing several times at the detectives, before eventually shrugging and falling silent in the face of his client's insistence.

'Ok,' said Rawmarsh, turning back to the detectives. 'Me and Gerry were at the quarry to steal the eggs.'

Harris tried to conceal his jubilation: he could not shake the feeling that the admission was more important than any involvement in the death of Paul de Luca. Nor, if the truth be told, had he tried particularly hard to do so.

'But,' added Rawmarsh quickly, 'that is far as it goes. Your witness has got it wrong about us meeting de Luca. We didn't know he was going to be there and we didn't see him. I ain't seen him for weeks, in fact.'

'So there had been a falling out?' said Harris quickly.

'I didn't say that.'

'What was it about?' asked Gallagher.

'I ain't saying nothing but you can take it from me, it ain't got nothing to do with his murder. And neither have we. If you say de Luca took the eggs, we'll have to take your word for it. It weren't no secret that they were there. Everyone knew about them, it was just a case of who got there first.'

The detectives eyed him for a few moments: Eddy Rawmarsh had rapidly recovered from his momentary unease and had delivered the statement in an assured, matter-of-fact manner. Now, ignoring his lawyer's unhappy expression, he stared at the officers as if challenging them to dispute his words. For their part, the detectives were uncomfortably aware that they had nothing with which to do so.

'Perhaps,' said Harris, standing up and smiling thinly as William Hadleigh flinched again, 'we should try to jog Mr Hopson's memory.'

'Just don't hit him,' said Rawmarsh nastily.

'He should be so lucky,' said the inspector, his voice floating back from the corridor.

He and his sergeant were approaching the station's other interview room when they saw Alison Butterfield walking rapidly down the corridor towards them.

'Have you got a minute, guv?' she asked.

'It's going to have to wait,' said the inspector, not breaking his stride.

'But this could be…'

'Later,' said the inspector, brushing past her.

'But I've got something interesting about…'

'I said later!' said Harris irritably and disappeared round the corner.

Gallagher winked at her then followed the inspector. Butterfield shook her head.

'Typical,' she muttered. 'Bloody typical.'

* * *

Sitting in the interview room, Gerald Hopson presented a pitiful sight, shaking and perspiring profusely

59

as he eyed the two detectives with a fearful expression when they took their seats at the table. Beside him, Ella Reynolds presented a calmer picture, although she did keep shooting concerned glances over at her panicking client. It was, thought Harris, the first time he had seen her display any sense that there could be cracks in the armour. *What kind of armour?* the chief inspector wondered idly as he tried to keep his eyes off the hint of cleavage afforded by the solicitor's shimmering pale blue blouse. Damn, he thought, keep your mind on the job. Think of Scoot, think of Scoot gnawing away at a dead rabbit. That should do it. The inspector noticed Reynolds watching him: was it his imagination or was there a twinkle in her eye? He dismissed the thought and glanced down at his notes on the table.

'Well, Mr Hopson,' he said, 'it does rather seem that we have a problem here. I say we, what I should have said is you, of course.'

'What do you mean?' said Hopson, displaying his nerves as his voice rose slightly, 'I have not done anything wrong.'

'Yes, so you keep saying. Unfortunately for you, Eddy Rawmarsh has just confirmed that the two of you were in the quarry yesterday. We also have a statement from someone else which also puts the two of you with Paul de Luca. The very day he was murdered, oddly enough. Now isn't that interesting?'

Hopson's eyes widened in horror. 'Murdered?' he croaked. 'I thought he fell?'

Ella Reynolds raised an eyebrow.

'Oh, didn't I mention that? Silly me,' said Harris, flicking through the papers with studious care until he produced a fax. 'Ah, here it is. Yes, according to the pathologist, it is more than likely that someone stoved the poor man's head in.'

'But I thought he fell,' repeated Hopson quietly.

'Was that your story?' asked Harris. 'Seems like you and Eddy are in deep trouble.'

'Jesus Christ,' moaned Hopson, burying his head in his hands.

'You'll need more than that to convince a magistrate,' said Reynolds, giving the inspector a sly look. 'Even one in a backwater like this.'

Gallagher smiled slightly as he noticed the inspector's irritated expression. If there was one thing that irked Harris it was the suggestion that rural police officers were in some way inferior to their urban colleagues. Gallagher knew the consequences of making such comments only too well and he suspected Ella Reynolds had said it deliberately.

'That is a risk we are prepared to take,' said Harris with restraint. 'We'll clear the sheep out of the courtroom first, of course, Ms Reynolds. You can't hear a thing the prosecution says with all that bleating.'

Reynolds inclined her head slightly in recognition of the joke.

'Besides,' continued Harris, 'there is also the question of the feud between Eddy Rawmarsh and our Mr de Luca.'

'Feud?' asked Reynolds quickly. 'What feud?'

'Ask Mr Hopson.'

Her composure finally disturbed, Ella Reynolds leaned over and whispered something to her client, who nodded dumbly.

'I think,' said Reynolds, 'that my client would like to make a written statement.'

Leaving Gallagher to oversee the process, the inspector strode out of the interview room to be met by the news that there was a visitor. He walked down to the front of the station and peeked through the reception area glass frontage. Even though he had not seen him for several years, there was no mistaking Paul de Luca's younger brother: just eighteen months separated them. Aged in his mid-forties, Robert was squat and muscular, with curly black hair and a swarthy complexion, and was dressed in jeans and a smart black windcheater. Harris watched him pace restlessly around the waiting room, hands gesticulating and lips moving, almost as if he was rehearsing something. The inspector walked into the reception area and extended a hand.

'Robert,' he said.

De Luca turned then his face broke into a smile.

'Hawk,' he said, as the men shook hands. 'I was hoping it would be you. Long time, no see.'

'A pity it could not be in more pleasant circumstances.'

Robert de Luca's face clouded over and, as Harris gestured for him to enter the side room, the inspector thought he saw tears glistening in his eyes. Harris felt surprise: he knew that the brothers had not been particularly close, increasingly growing apart down the years, separated by Paul's affinity for crime. He knew that when they were younger there had been frequent rows about Paul's lifestyle and the idea that Robert would grieve for his dead brother took the inspector aback slightly. Perhaps it reminded Robert de Luca of what could have been, thought the inspector as he sat down and looked across the table at his visitor.

'Was it an accident?' asked Robert.

'The pathologist thinks he may have been assaulted.'

'I guess that's not a complete surprise. Any idea who did it?'

Harris decided to choose his words carefully, mindful that he had little evidence and that Curtis was increasingly twitchy on the subject. The last thing Harris needed was unguarded words getting back to Ella Reynolds.

'I have two men in custody,' he said.

'Are we by any chance talking about Rawmarsh and Hopson?'

'How do you know that?'

'I knew they were going after the eggs,' said Robert. 'Paul rang me a few days ago – wanted to talk about Megan's birthday present, it was the first time I had heard from him in months – and he mentioned it then. He said he was coming up here on his own – he'd fallen out with the others.'

'What about?'

De Luca hesitated.

'I'll find out anyway,' said Harris.

'Yes, I suppose you will. According to Paul, Eddy Rawmarsh had got it into his head that my brother had been grassing to the police. Something to do with stolen cars.'

'And had he?'

'You knew Paul,' said de Luca with a slight smile. 'He would not give you lot a cold.'

Harris nodded: he knew Paul de Luca only too well. Remembered how violent could be his moods, how criminal could be his intent, how persuasive could be his ways. He remembered how even as a young man, Paul seemed determined to flout authority and how on so many occasions, he had been vehement in his distaste for the police. Now, as he often did, Harris wondered where it had all come from. Certainly not from the brothers' father, an Italian immigrant who had come over in the post-war years to run a garage in Levton Bridge. Harris remembered Gianni as a hard-working, honest man and his wife as a typical Italian matriarchal figure with a strong line in discipline. He knew that Paul's criminal ways had been a great disappointment to them both. Robert, on the other hand, had steered clear of criminal temptation and had instead taken over the business when his father retired, only to close it and move to Manchester when his parents died within eighteen months of each other. The building had stood derelict for years but had recently been bought, then bulldozed to make way for apartments, the first in Levton Bridge.

'I wanted to say something,' said Robert, voice trembling with emotion. 'I did not get on with Paul – that's no secret around these parts – but I still want you to find his killer. He was still family. I will offer you all the help I can.'

'You can start by identifying the body.'

'Do I have to?'

'You're the next of kin. Sorry.'

'Where is he?' asked Robert.

'Roxham Hospital. I'll get one of my officers to take you. She's called Alison Butterfield.'

'Is she pretty?' asked de Luca.

'I wouldn't kick her out of bed to get to you.'

'Have you tried?' said Robert with an impish grin.

Harris decided not to answer the question.

'One more thing before you go,' he said as Robert stood up. 'Your brother must have made a few enemies in his time and I really do not have much to link Rawmarsh and Hopson to his death – any idea who else might have had it in for him?'

'I kept out of all that.'

'Nevertheless…'

'Sorry, Hawk. Paul's world was Paul's world and I wanted no part of it. I made my father a promise and I stuck to it. There comes a time when a man has to choose the path down which he will walk and I chose mine.' He glanced at his watch. 'Listen, can we get this over with? I really do need to get back home to Manchester tonight.'

'Yeah, ok,' said Harris, following him to the door. 'Do we know where to find you?'

'Your sergeant does.' De Luca fished around in his coat pocket before handing over a business card. 'We live in the house next to the garage.'

'Thanks,' said Harris, showing him into the reception area and extending a hand. 'I'll get Constable Butterfield to come down for you.'

'Just find who did this,' said de Luca.

Chapter six

'There's more to the disappearance of Jimmy Roscoe than meets the eye,' said Gallagher, glancing across at the desk occupied by the only other officer in the CID room. 'It just does not *feel* like an accident.'

'I thought the boss told you to concentrate on Rawmarsh and Hopson,' said Robbie Graham, who had walked in a few moments before and was now unwrapping a belated lunch.

'He did, but I got a funny feeling about this one.'

'It's the governor's funny feelings you should be more worried about.'

'Not sure he does funny,' said Gallagher.

It was 2pm, an hour since a grumbling Alison Butterfield had been told to take Robert de Luca to Roxham Hospital to identify his brother's body. She had tried to tell the detective chief inspector her news about Corbett but he had brushed aside her attempts and had left the room without further word. Struggling into her coat once the inspector had gone, Butterfield had angrily declined to tell Matty Gallagher what was so important and stalked from the room, muttering something about 'not being a bloody taxi service'. Since her departure, calm had returned to the room as the sergeant sat alone, waiting for phone calls and reading through the reports into the disappearance of Jimmy Roscoe until the return of Graham, a tousled-headed man in his twenties who had been seconded to CID several weeks previously.

'According to this,' said Gallagher, holding up the Prison Service report, 'Jimmy absolutely hated being locked up. That's why they let him out early. It made him ill.'

'Diddums.'

'That's what I thought but it appears they did it because they'd already had one inmate die a few weeks before.'

'That's careless.'

'More than that, Robbie. There was a big inquiry about it – turned out someone in the kitchens put glass in his food.'

'Charming,' said Graham, taking a large bite from her ham sandwich. 'Was Jimmy involved?'

'Doesn't look like it.'

'Perhaps someone at Mandy's Bakery was,' said Graham, pulling a face. 'If this has ever been near a pig, I'm a Dutchman.'

Gallagher smiled: you couldn't help liking Robbie Graham. His cheery demeanour was a pleasant antidote to the complaining Butterfield and the surly chief inspector. Not to mention the rampaging superintendent, who was at force headquarters down in the valley and had rung the office three times in the past hour and a half, looking for Harris. Gallagher's vague replies had only served to infuriate the commander even further and on the final occasion, he had slammed the phone down.

'So how come you think his disappearance is iffy?' asked Graham, taking another bite and reaching for his can of Coke.

'Not sure yet,' said Gallagher and glanced down at the documents in front of him. 'But the reports from the time read like someone who did not want to know.'

The sergeant glanced up at the clock on the CID room wall, swore, hurriedly pulled on his coat and got to his feet.

'Got to go,' he said, heading for the door.

'Why the hurry?'

'I want to avoid the super. He's driving me bonkers.'

'Say no more, matey-boy,' grinned Graham.

However, as Gallagher walked briskly into the corridor, he saw Curtis striding purposefully towards him.

'Shit,' murmured the sergeant. He knew that look, a man on a mission. The sergeant forced out a smile. 'Hallo, sir, how are?'

'Where's Harris?'

'I don't know, sir.'

Which was true. After dispatching Butterfield to escort Robert de Luca, Jack Harris had gone into a short, but fractious, meeting in which he had informed Ella Reynolds and William Hadleigh that he would be keeping their clients in for another night on suspicion of murder. Having watched them storm furiously from the room, Hadleigh threatening all sorts of dire repercussions, Harris had gone back to his office and given a low whistle to Scoot, who was curled up under the desk. With the dog at his heels, the inspector had walked briskly past the CID room, waving away questions from Gallagher.

Abandoned to face the angry lawyers, Gallagher had rung the inspector's mobile twice since then but the phone appeared to have been switched off. Guessing that Curtis would be on his way back from headquarters and that it would not take long for the solicitors to complain to him once he arrived at Levton Bridge, Gallagher had decided that he could risk tying up some loose ends before heading out to conduct some inquiries. Now, standing in front of the baleful superintendent, it seemed he had got his timing wrong. Badly wrong.

'What do you mean, you don't know where he is?' said Curtis suspiciously, fixing the sergeant with a hard stare.

'He said something about going out on inquiries.'

'What kind of inquiries?'

'Not sure, sir.'

'Why not? You're his bloody sergeant.'

'Yes, that's true, sir, but he doesn't necessarily tell me everything he is doing.'

'Join the club,' said the superintendent sourly. 'Well, while he's swanning about, I've had the lawyers banging on my door again, demanding to know on what grounds you are keeping Rawmarsh and Hopson locked up. I'd only been in the building thirty seconds. Do you have any idea what is happening, by the vaguest of chances?'

Gallagher cursed inwardly, furious that the chief inspector had placed him in such a situation. At a time when the sergeant was trying to persuade the commander to approve his transfer request to an urban division, such embarrassments hardly helped his cause. The superintendent's thunderous expression suggested that this was not the time to bring the subject up again.

Curtis noticed the sergeant's hesitation.

'Well?' he repeated, 'why are you keeping them in?'

'Because,' began Gallagher tentatively, 'both of them have admitted to being in the quarry yesterday. They were after the eagle eggs, you see, and the guv'nr...'

'Forget the bloody eggs!' exclaimed Curtis angrily. 'They have got nothing to do with this!'

'Actually, there might be a link, sir. The DCI says most wildlife criminals are involved in other types of crime. He says it's a case of anything to make money and that if...'

'You're not in one of his sodding seminars now, Sergeant! Have you got anything whatsoever to link these men to the murder?'

'Well, we do have a witness who said he saw de Luca with the other two yesterday. Geordie Carroll says…'

'Another birdwatcher,' snorted Curtis.

'Yes, but…'

'And what's more, I hear you don't find his account entirely convincing anyway,' said Curtis, eying him keenly. 'Is that right?'

Wondering how the superintendent had heard about his doubts, Gallagher nodded reluctantly. That was the problem with small-town stations, he reflected darkly, you couldn't keep anything secret.

'Look, Sergeant, I can't afford us to mess this up so unless you can come up with something better than a few tenuous theories, I suggest they are both released on bail.'

'Well, that's a decision for the DCI really and…'

'I bloody well know that, Sergeant! But as usual, Jack Harris has gone missing. Presumably with that blessed cur of his,' and Curtis eyed Gallagher's coat dubiously. 'And where might you be going?'

'A new line of inquiry,' said Gallagher evasively.

'Perhaps, the DCI has asked you to pop out to get some dog biscuits?' said the superintendent, turning on his heel. 'Just tell Jack Harris that I want to see him.'

Gallagher glumly watched him stride back down the corridor, sighed and headed, gratefully, in the opposite direction. Ten minutes later, he was sitting in the tidy front room of Geordie Carroll's bungalow on the edge of Levton Bridge. Wildlife magazines were piled up on the floor in one corner of the room and the somewhat ramshackle bookcase standing against the far wall was so crammed with books about birds that it seemed that they might overbalance at any time and spill out across the carpet.

Gallagher had not meant to visit Carroll when he left the police station, bound for Chapel Ebton and Jimmy Roscoe's aged mother, but the pointed comments from Curtis had brought Carroll back to the front of his mind again. Convinced that he was holding something back, and finding himself passing the end of the road where he lived, the sergeant had impulsively yanked on the steering wheel and pulled up outside the bungalow. Now, sitting on the sofa, he found himself wondering, somewhat uncomfortably, exactly what he was going to say. He knew that anger had driven him there and he was beginning to regret the decision. From the kitchen came the rattle of cups and in walked Geordie Carroll, bearing a tray.

'Tea,' he announced, setting it down on a small table between them.

Matty Gallagher watched Carroll pour, the pause allowing the detective to survey him more carefully. The gathering in the quarry had been the first time Gallagher had met him and his perusal now suggested a man of contradictions. His wiry frame clearly indicated someone who kept himself fit – Gallagher knew that Carroll spent most of his time walking the hills in his role as a national park ranger – but his thinning grey hair and wispy beard showed streaks of yellow, a testament to a lifetime of heavy smoking. Indeed, he could hear Carroll's slightly laboured breathing as he poured the tea.

'I sense that you do not like me,' said Carroll, sitting down in his armchair.

'What makes you think that?'

'There is an absence of the warmth that so characterises Jack.'

'Jack who?'

Carroll raised an eyebrow.

'Not Jack Harris surely?' said the sergeant.

'Perhaps you do not know your chief inspector as well as you should.'

The voice had a mocking edge to it and, acutely aware that he was being outmanoeuvred, and irritated at Gallagher's tone, Gallagher reached into his suit jacket pocket and produced his notebook.

'I was wondering,' he said, 'if you had remembered anything else that may be of use in our inquiries?'

'Was my statement not sufficient? I felt it was very precise.'

'It was very useful,' nodded Gallagher, reaching for his tea, 'and it certainly put the wind up Eddy Rawmarsh.'

'Which was the intention, of course. But I suspect that you are not here to talk about my statement,' and he eyed the sergeant closely. 'I suspect that you have come about something else.'

'In a way,' said Gallagher, selecting his words carefully: he guessed Harris would react badly if word got back that his sergeant was pressuring one of his closest friends without the evidence to back it up. 'It's what is missing from your statement, Mr Carroll. When I asked you where you were in the hour before you saw the men, you said you were watching the eagles' nest.'

'Which I was. We set up a vantage point on the far side of the quarry. I told you all this last time.'

'The trouble is, there is no one to confirm that. You normally watch in pairs, I understand, but on this occasion you were alone.'

'Like I said last time we spoke, James Scotton was due to be with me but had to cancel at the last minute. His wife has been ill and he had to take her to the doctor's.'

The answer was given calmly, Geordie Carroll continuing to eye the sergeant carefully, as if seeking some kind of reaction. In the few seconds of silence, Gallagher did the same. Studying the angular face, pronounced cheekbones and eyes that gleamed bright and blue, Gallagher found himself thinking of a hawk. A predator eying up its prey. The image startled, and disturbed him.

'Anything else?' asked Carroll. 'I am rather b…'

'You also claim that after you saw Rawmarsh and Hopson with de Luca, you walked across the fell until you could get a signal on your mobile, then you called the DCI.'

'Reception is notoriously poor in the quarry. Look, Sergeant, what is your problem?' There was the first hint of irritation in Carroll's voice. 'I find your insinuations somewhat tiresome. Am I a suspect?'

'No, of course not, I am just wondering why you did not confront the three of them there and then, in the quarry. I mean, you could have saved the eggs, surely. Returned them to the nest even. How come you did nothing?'

Carroll reached for his cup of tea and took a sip. For a few moments, the sergeant wondered if he had not heard the question. Gallagher was about to repeat it when Carroll looked at him.

'Did you ever meet Paul de Luca, Sergeant?'

'No, I didn't.'

'If you had, you would not have asked me that question. It would probably have been me lying in the mortuary if I had revealed myself to him. Ask Hawk about him. In fact, ask anyone about Paul de Luca. They'll tell you what he was like. There's few around here will mourn his passing.'

'Yes but…'

'It all happened as I said in my statement,' and Carroll's voice hardened and he placed his cup down with a bang, sending tea slopping across the table. 'Any attempt to cast aspersions on my good character will be robustly defended and I will not hesitate to make a formal complaint to your Superintendent Curtis. Perhaps you ought to remember that, Sergeant.'

Carroll stood up and gestured to the door.

'Now, I would appreciate it if you left,' he said.

Gallagher hesitated for a moment then nodded and walked out into the narrow hallway.

'Just one thing,' he said, opening the front door and ignoring Carroll's exasperated expression, 'does the name Jimmy Roscoe mean anything to you? He went missing on the fells fifteen years ago.'

'He will not be the last to go missing on the hills. Worth remembering that. Good day, Sergeant Gallagher.'

Standing on the driveway as the door slammed behind him, Matty Gallagher could not help thinking that Carroll's parting comment sounded like a threat.

* * *

Jack Harris parked the car in the middle of the village and sat for a few moments surveying the rows of cottages. Getting out, he noticed a white-haired man walking down the road towards him. The man smiled as he recognised the inspector.

'Hawk,' he said delightedly, 'how the hell are you?'

His face fell as Harris declined to shake the offered hand of friendship.

'I take it's not a personal visit?' he said.

'I am afraid this is business, Davy,' said the inspector, gesturing towards the house. 'You and I need to talk.'

* * *

The confrontation with Geordie Carroll stayed with Gallagher as he made the half-hour drive to Chapel Ebton, turning off the main road and into the tiny village, which huddled around a bridge over a bubbling stream, the road then winding its way up into the hills and out of sight. Follow it far enough north through the valley and Gallagher knew that you would eventually cross the Scottish border. Not that he had ever done it: he was already far enough north for his liking. The village itself comprised no more than fifty slate-grey cottages, the derelict eponymous Methodist Chapel, all moss and crumbling stone, and a boarded-up shop whose owners had sold up some years before, blaming the opening of a supermarket in the nearest large town.

Getting out of his car, Gallagher looked around him bleakly. These places were dying on their feet, he thought. Glancing up to the hills, which stretched out beneath a rapidly darkening sky as the rain clouds gathered once more, the sergeant realised that it was at times like this that he missed London more than ever. It was the silence. Having always lived in London, Gallagher had never known silence: even lying in bed in the middle of the night there would be the hum of traffic and the distant sound of voices as revellers staggered home from the city's pubs and clubs. Now Gallagher sat and listened to the roaring silence and sighed. He was due a few days' leave and it was time for a trip home, he thought. Grab a few jars with some old friends and see his dad.

The sergeant knew that Jack Harris would see the scene differently if he were standing there. He knew that the DCI would wax lyrical about the view, and bang on endlessly about connections with the landscape, one of his recurrent themes, but Matty Gallagher could see none of it. There were times when he wished he could, but not many and he did not wish very hard. Thought of the inspector brought forth a scowl from the sergeant. Apart from mulling over the conversation with Geordie Carroll during the drive to Chapel Ebton, the sergeant had also brooded on the way Harris had abandoned him to his humiliating dressing-down by Curtis. It wasn't the first time that had happened, thought Gallagher darkly as he locked the car door and started walking towards the nearest row of cottages. He reached into his coat pocket and produced his notebook, then, having found the right page, sought out number nine Chapel Row.

'Even God's given up on them,' he murmured, his eyes ranging along from the terrace to the dilapidated church at the far end.

Number nine was a dimly-lit cottage with sagging gutters, crumbling brickwork and a piece of wire sticking out where the bell push had once been. Had Gallagher not glanced through the grimy window and seen a hunched shape sitting by the fire, he might have assumed the place was empty. The sergeant banged loudly on the door: the noise seemed to reverberate round the hills, its resonance catching him by surprise. Receiving no reply, he hammered again, noticing twitching curtains at a house a little further down the terrace. When he turned to look, however, the curtains stilled. It took a long time for the door of number nine to open and the sergeant was starting to contemplate whether or not to force his way in to see if Jimmy Roscoe's mother was alright when there was the sound of a latch being pulled back. The door swung open to reveal a stooped, grey-haired woman wearing a dull brown dress and a tattered shawl draped over her shoulders. It had probably once been red, thought the sergeant, but it was difficult to tell, so faded were the colours.

'Edith Roscoe?' asked the sergeant.

'Whatever you are selling, I don't want it,' she said, surveying him suspiciously over her spectacles.

'I am Detective Sergeant Gallagher,' he said, flashing his card. 'Can I come in?'

She studied the card closely but did not move aside.

'Why?' she asked.

'It's about Jimmy.'

For a moment, Gallagher thought the woman was going to close the door slam in his face but she gave a slight nod and stepped back, gesturing for him to enter. The sergeant walked into the living room, a gloomy, cluttered affair with a threadbare sofa, a large dark wood dresser and a coal fire that sputtered feebly. There was a strange musty smell that Gallagher could not quite place and what little light there was came from a shabby standard lamp in a corner of the room.

'Sit down,' said Edith, gesturing to the sofa. 'I hope this won't take long. I never miss Countdown.'

Gallagher lowered himself gingerly onto the sofa: it looked as if it might collapse at any moment.

'Thank you,' he said.

'What about Jimmy?' she asked as she sat down on the armchair, wincing at the pain from her right leg, which she reached out to straighten once she had settled herself. 'Not that you lot ever seemed bothered about what happened when he disappeared.'

Gallagher realised that he had overlooked the possibility that she might feel angry that the police had failed to find her son, that he might be dealing with wounds that had not healed. He recalled the inspector's warning and realised what it had meant. *Was he wasting everyone's time?* This was a time for sensitivity, Gallagher told himself. He had already irritated Geordie Carroll; hacking off two people in the same afternoon would not go down well should Superintendent Curtis get to hear about it – and his experience was that, in the close hill communities surrounding Levton Bridge, he always did. When the sergeant did not reply to her question, Edith Roscoe looked shrewdly at him.

'I assume you are here because of Paul de Luca?'

The comment took him aback. 'And why should that be?'

'Well, no one has asked about Jimmy for fifteen years then suddenly Paul dies and you turn up. Why else would you be interested?'

Gallagher nodded.

'Your son knew Paul de Luca, I think?' he asked.

'They all did.'

'All?'

'I was expecting Jack Harris,' she said.

'I gather he knew him,' nodded the sergeant.

'A little more than that, Sergeant. They went to school together.'

'They did?'

'I am surprised he did not mention it. Mind, he did have his moments so perhaps it's not that much of surprise.'

'It is to me,' murmured Gallagher. 'Where was this then?'

'Levton Bridge Primary. Jack was there at the same time as the Luca boys and my two,' and she nodded to a corner table. 'See?'

Gallagher walked across the room and saw a faded school picture in a battered frame. He picked it up and, scanning the lines of beaming children standing to attention in the playground, recognised on the back row a young Jack Harris. Surveying the glowering expression, the sergeant chuckled. Despite the passage of time, nothing had changed. Next to Harris stood another boy, swarthy even at such a young age: Paul de Luca. It could be no one else. On the front row was an older child with similar heavy features. Robert, decided Gallagher. Had to be.

'Jimmy?' asked Gallagher, holding up the picture and turning to look at Edith. 'Is he there?'

'Next to Jack. The one with the snotty nose.'

Gallagher turned and saw her smiling.

'He always had a snotty nose,' she said. 'You have probably worked out which one is Paul de Luca. He was mean even in those days. His brother was different, a lovely lad was Robert. I often wish he had been Jimmy's brother instead.'

'And after Jimmy left school,' said Gallagher, putting the picture down and returning to the sofa, 'did he keep in touch with the others? Did he keep in touch with Paul de Luca?'

'They may have met each other. I don't really know.'

'I assume that's how Jimmy got into crime?'

'I never asked him how it happened.'

'But you knew that Paul de Luca was a criminal?'

'I may be ninety-three but I'm not stupid, Sergeant.' There was an edge to her voice. 'Of course I knew but I blame Garry for what happened. He started stealing cars and got Jimmy involved.'

'Is Garry on the picture?' asked Gallagher, looking over at the corner table again.

'No, he couldn't even turn up for that,' and she snorted. 'The police found him in an amusement arcade in Roxham. Typical. I gave up counting how many times he got expelled. His father disowned him, you know. Broke his heart.'

She stared into the fire. 'Broke his heart.'

'And Jimmy?' asked Gallagher softly. 'Did your husband disown Jimmy?'

She shook her head.

'But he was a criminal as well,' said the sergeant.

'Jimmy was different,' she said, looking at him sharply. 'Garry was the one that led him into trouble.'

'And where is Garry now, Mrs Roscoe?'

'I haven't seen him for years – and I don't want to, neither. Last I heard he was in London.'

It seemed to Gallagher that, as she stared once more into the sputtering embers of the fire, there was a sadness in her eyes. The sadness that could only be felt by a mother, he thought. He had seen that look before, from his own childhood, from those times when his mother was summoned by the headteacher to account for his latest transgression – and there had been many of them. Too many. Even now, years later, the recollection caused Matty Gallagher to feel pangs of guilt and, as always, he wished that he had found the words to tell his mother how sorry he was before she died. He remembered her now as he sat watching Edith fighting against the strong emotions coursing through her frail body.

'Can you cast your mind back to the day Jimmy disappeared?' asked the sergeant.

'Why should I?' she said. The sadness had gone as suddenly as it had appeared, to be replaced by hostility, almost as if she regretted letting down her guard to a stranger.

'It may be of use.'

Edith watched him produce his pocket book and fish around in his suit jacket for a pen, then nodded her assent. She stood up, wincing with pain as she did so, and hobbled over to the mantelpiece.

'That's the last picture of Jimmy,' she said, reaching up to take down another faded colour photograph, which she handed to the sergeant.

Gallagher felt surprise as he looked at the tall bushy-haired man leaning against the bridge in the heart of the village. All rosy cheeks and big vacant smile, and dressed in a chunky blue sweater and green baggy cords, Gallagher had expected someone small and weasely. He remembered Harris talking about how Jimmy only started growing when he was fourteen. Boy, how he had started growing, thought Gallagher. Instinctively, he glanced over at the little lad on the school photograph.

'He was a late developer,' said Edith, reading his thoughts. 'Mind, he did not look like that on the day he vanished.'

'No?'

'He lost a lot of weight when he was inside,' said Edith, replacing the picture on mantelpiece then wincing once again at the pain from her leg as she sat down. 'That's why he came home, to get himself well, but Garry wouldn't leave him alone.'

'How come?'

'Garry came up the day he got out of prison. Wanted Jimmy to go back with him but he told Garry he wanted nothing more of it. Knocked his brother to the ground.'

'Really?' said the sergeant, sitting forward in his chair. 'Was this the day he disappeared?'

'The week before. Garry went back to Liverpool after that. Jimmy was really upset by what had happened. I had never seen him like that.'

'So what happened on the day he vanished?'

She hesitated, struggling once more to control her emotions, and finally began speaking in a quiet voice.

'Jimmy was going to walk over to one of the farms,' she said. 'He'd heard that they had some labouring work.'

'I thought Jimmy was a mechanic?'

'After he got out of prison, he said he would never work with cars again. The labouring job would have been a new start for him.'

'But he never came back?'

The sergeant saw tears glistening in her rheumy eyes.

'You know the answer to that,' she said.

'Yes, I do,' nodded Gallagher. 'Yes, I do. I'm sorry, silly question. Can I ask you another one?'

'Another silly one?' she asked with a slight smile.

'I'll try to make it sensible, Mrs Roscoe.'

'Call me Edith, pet.'

'Ok, Edith, thank you. I wanted to ask if you think Jimmy's death was an accident? People seem to think he fell down a mine shaft.'

'Jimmy was born in this cottage,' she said, and held her hand close to the floor, 'and he was walking these hills with his Da from the day he was this high. He knew every inch of the fells. There's no way he fell down a mine shaft.'

Gallagher hesitated for a moment.

'Is there a chance,' he said eventually, 'that he did it deliberately?'

Her eyes flashed anger.

'No!' she said vehemently. 'Jimmy would never do that. Never, do you understand!'

'Ok, ok,' nodded the sergeant, 'but what's the alternative? I mean, there is absolutely nothing to suggest foul play in the report that PC Garbutt filed at the time. He didn't even mention the fight with Garry.'

'Davy Garbutt wasn't interested,' she said dismissively. 'More interested in a quiet life. His inspector did not seem interested either.'

'Can you remember who you saw?'

'I think his name was Corbett.'

'Ralph Corbett?'

'That's him. A very rude man.' She looked at him shrewdly. 'You seem to be asking a lot of questions. Are you re-opening the investigation into Jimmy's disappearance?'

Not for the first time in the conversation he was taken by surprise by the sharp ways of this elderly woman. 'Do you think I should?' he asked eventually.

'All I want is for you to find Jimmy,' she said, looking into the dying embers of the fire then turning dark eyes back to the detective, 'because until you do, I cannot lay my little boy to rest.'

Gallagher looked up at Jimmy Roscoe beaming down from the mantelpiece then glanced over at the school picture. The young Jack Harris glowered out at him and the sergeant felt a tingling sensation run down his spine. A few minutes later, Gallagher was leaving the cottage; having lost track of time, he was surprised to see how dark it had become on the hills. He was just about to unlock his car when the curtain flickered in the window of the cottage further down the row. The sergeant thought for a moment then walked along the street and rang on the doorbell. A grey-haired woman in her sixties answered it.

'Excuse me, I could not help noticing that you have been watching me.' He flashed his ID. 'Why?'

'We look out for each other up here,' said the woman. 'Edith has not been well and…'

'Did you know Jimmy?'

'Why?' The woman seemed keen to close the door.

'Just routine inquiries. Do you know anything about what happened to him?'

'Such things,' she said firmly, 'are best left to the past.'

The door closed and the sergeant started to walk back down the street. As he did so, he noticed through the woman's window that she was on the telephone.

'Woollybacks,' he murmured.

He had just unlocked the car when his phone rang. It was Superintendent Curtis.

'Have you heard from Harris yet?' asked the commander in a harsh voice. 'The lawyers have been having a go at me again.'

'Have you tried his mobile?' said Gallagher, struggling to cup the phone under his chin as he clambered into the car.

'I can't get an answer,' said Curtis irritably.

'Maybe it's out of reception range, sir.'

'Well, I seem to be able to get you alright.'

'Yes,' said Gallagher gloomily as he lowered himself into the driver's seat, 'yes, it appears that you can, sir.'

The man watched the sergeant's car pull away from the cottage and head out onto the main valley road, its headlights puncturing the gathering darkness. Standing just outside the village, concealed behind a wall, the man had witnessed the sergeant's arrival with interest and had resolved to stay where he was until the detective left. A woman walking a dog had passed him at one point and had given him a strange look, her stride slowing momentarily. The man had reached into his rucksack and produced a map, which he proceeded to study intently. The gesture seemed to reassure her and the women and her dog continued on to one of the cottages. Now, the man watched Gallagher leave, waiting for his car's headlights to fade from sight, before turning and heading up into the hills where he soon vanished into the evening gloom.

Chapter seven

After his meeting, Jack Harris drove for another few minutes to the next village where he got out of the car – he had borrowed an unmarked vehicle to avoid arousing suspicions – and glanced furtively around. To his relief, the high street was deserted. For a few moments, he stood and stared up wistfully at the surrounding hills. With a sigh, he pushed his way into The Half Moon, Scoot trotting happily at his heels. Pubs with Jack Harris usually meant a saucer of beer. The old coaching house at the far end of Cleighton was quiet. Harris knew it would be – it was only 3.15pm – and the inspector had chosen the location because, situated more than an hour's drive from Levton Bridge, the village was just over the force's southern boundary, meaning less chance of being spotted by one of his officers. Harris knew that there would be trouble should word get back to Curtis that he had been meeting Graham Leckie. Even though Leckie's call had not been about wildlife, the inspector knew the commander would automatically assume that it was.

As the inspector had predicted, the lounge was empty, apart from a bored-looking bar manager wiping glasses and an elderly man sitting in one of the window seats.

Harris gave him a quick glance – he sensed that the man would be nursing his pint for a while – then nodded to the bar tender and walked across the lounge, past the shining horse brasses and the 19th Century oil paintings of sheep. The inspector smiled as he spotted a figure sitting next to the fire. A tall, lean man with thinning black hair and a pronounced five o'clock shadow, Graham Leckie was dressed in dark trousers and a blue shirt, having gone home to change out of his uniform before driving up the M6 from Manchester. He knew that Harris would not want to draw attention to their meeting.

'Hawk,' he said, standing up and extending a hand. 'How's it hanging?'

'It won't be hanging at all if Curtis has anything to do with it,' said Harris sourly, then nodded at the bar. 'Drinky-poo?'

'Aye, just a half. Not that local stuff, though. I farted all the way back last time. Had to fumigate the car when I got home.'

Harris chuckled and went to get the drinks. Returning a minute or so later, he sat down next to Leckie. The barman came over and placed a saucer of beer down for Scoot. Harris nodded his thanks.

'I deserve this,' said the inspector, holding his glass up and watching the way the whisky glinted in the firelight.

'Not making any headway?'

'Not enough.'

'Then perhaps I can help. I did a bit of asking round, like you said. There's been a load of high-end cars nicked in our area – nothing under £25,000 – and our auto-crime boys reckon they are being driven down to a chop shop in London. Word is that Paul de Luca was one of those involved at the Manchester end.'

'Now that's interesting,' said Harris. 'Is it asking too much to put Rawmarsh in there as well?'

'If he was involved, he was very much on the fringes, but Paul de Luca, he was right in the thick of it. It's all very

84

hush-hush but our lads have been working with the Met on this one for several months. I've got some names for you to call and our DI says you can give him a bell any time you want.'

'Thanks for that.'

'There's more,' said Leckie, glancing round and lowering his voice. 'Three weeks ago, our lot picked up some rumours that de Luca had turned grass. He had supplied the getaway car for a robbery but the job went wrong. Couple of uniforms stumbled upon it – pure accident – but the gang decided someone on the inside had grassed them up and fingers pointed at de Luca for some reason.'

'We'd heard rumours about some kind of a falling out,' said Harris, 'but I can't see it, myself.'

'What does it matter? The point is that the gang thought it was true. Anyway, de Luca went off the radar but resurfaced in Manchester city centre a few days ago. There was a dust up in a pub between him and a couple of our local bad lads. Nasty stuff, apparently.'

'Anyone hurt?'

'Word is that one of them tried to glass de Luca. Usual stuff, though, by the time our lot arrived, they had all gone and no one in the pub had seen anything.'

'And now Paul de Luca's dead,' said Harris.

'And now Paul de Luca's dead. Maybe this is a good old-fashioned hit. Maybe the eggs were simply a way of getting him somewhere they could kill him.'

'Which puts Rawmarsh in up to his neck,' said Harris.

'Maybe it does but no one has mentioned his name. Don't look like that, you know I'd like to see him locked up as much as you but we have to face facts here.'

'You sound like Curtis.'

'Maybe he's got a point then,' said Leckie and laughed as he saw Harris scowling.

'Besides,' added Leckie, 'there's another name I want to drop in. Comes from up your way, has got form and is known to be an associate of Paul de Luca. Chap called Garry Roscoe.'

'Garry Roscoe,' said Harris with a gleam in his eye.

'You know him?'

'Oh, yeah, I know Garry Roscoe. In fact,' Harris took a sip of his whisky, 'I've been waiting for Garry Roscoe for a long, long time. If I can't get Eddy Rawmarsh, Garry Roscoe will do nicely.'

'Well, our DI reckons he is the main man at the London end. The Met lads have been watching him for weeks.'

'Thanks, matey-boy,' said Harris, clinking his glass on Leckie's. 'I owe you one.'

'In which case,' said Leckie, emptying his glass and breaking wind noisily, 'I guess it's time you delivered.'

* * *

Back at the police station late that afternoon, a thoughtful Matty Gallagher walked through dimly-lit, and largely deserted, corridors to the detective chief inspector's first floor office. He had decided on the drive back to Levton Bridge to be conciliatory with his colleague, realising that there were sensitive issues to be broached, but the sight of the chief inspector hunched over his desk, studying a number of documents and pointedly ignoring Gallagher's arrival, revived the sergeant's previous irritations.

'And where the hell have you been?' asked Gallagher. 'Curtis has been making my life a misery. Rung me three times on the way back here and what's more he…'

'I heard he had been giving you a hard time,' said Harris, without a hint of apology in his voice and still not looking up.

'Too true he has. In fact…'

'Rather like you did with Geordie Carroll earlier today,' said Harris, finally looking up. 'Thanks for running it past me first.'

'He's been onto you then?' said the sergeant, calming down slightly – he realised that he was on somewhat shaky ground.

'Said you all but accused him of killing Paul de Luca,' said Harris, gesturing for the sergeant to sit down. 'Care to explain yourself? Because if Geordie withdraws his statement in a fit of pique, and he is perfectly capable of doing just that, then we have nothing against Rawmarsh and Hopson and they'll walk for sure.'

'I reckoned he needed to answer some questions,' said Gallagher defensively. He then shot the inspector a sly look. 'As do you, guv.'

'Is that right?' said Harris calmly. 'And what questions would you like answering?'

'How about we start with why you never told me that you went to school with Paul de Luca?'

'It hardly seemed relevant,' shrugged Harris. 'Besides, it's no big secret, everyone knows everyone around here, it's part of living in a place like this. I've told you that enough times. So who told you?'

'Edith Roscoe.'

'I thought I told you do concentrate on Rawmarsh and Hopson.'

'Yeah, I know and I put loads of calls in and…'

'No matter,' said the inspector with a wave of the hand. 'How is the old goat?'

'Hacked off at us for failing to find her son.'

'I'm not surprised. In fact…' The inspector held up his pocket book, 'I popped in on Davy Garbutt this afternoon.'

'I thought you said I was wasting my time?'

'I can change my mind,' said Harris with the slightest of smiles. 'It's one of the privileges of rank. Besides, Davy tried to put me off re-opening the case – that's enough to get me thinking.'

'According to Jimmy's mum, he did a rubbish job.'

Although the sergeant's tone of voice was firm, belligerent even, it was also slightly guarded: everyone knew that Jack Harris disliked criticism of officers by their own colleagues. 'If we can't have faith in each other, how on earth can we expect the public to trust us?' he often said. Waiting for the same response now, Gallagher looked at Harris, defying him to challenge the statement. If the inspector wanted a fight, then the sergeant was in the mood to.

'I think she is probably right,' said Harris.

'You do?' said the sergeant, unable to conceal his surprise: like he always told other officers, it was a waste of time trying to read Jack Harris, you'd always end up getting it wrong.

'Can't help feeling that he was too eager to put it down as an accident,' said Harris. 'Besides, I know Davy Garbutt of old – anything for an easy life that one. Working up here can do that to you.'

Gallagher wondered if the irony of the comment was lost on the chief inspector. He decided not to ask.

'I guess,' he said, hesitating as he phrased his words carefully, 'the last thing he wants is someone digging up past failures once he has retired. And there's someone else who might feel the same way.'

'I wondered when you would get round to that. I take it Edith told you that Ralph Corbett was the inspector at the time.'

Gallagher nodded.

'So where are we then?' he asked. 'We can out Garry Roscoe and Paul de Luca together but can't connect de Luca to Jimmy's disappearance. What do we do now?'

'How do you fancy a trip to London?'

'Yeah, sure,' said Gallagher, his face lighting up. 'But why? Surely you need me up here.'

'Because,' and Harris reached for a piece of paper on his desk, 'that is where Jimmy Roscoe's toe-rag brother is living. I put a call into the Met officer handling the investigation into his latest chop shop: good job you told me what one was otherwise I would have come over as a real yokel. Mind, he's probably never seen a sheep.'

Gallagher looked at him ruefully. Harris slid the piece of paper across the desk. The sergeant saw that it was a faxed intelligence report from the Met's stolen cars squad: he even recognised the name of Danny Raine, the detective inspector with whom he had worked for six months before leaving the capital.

'As you can see,' said Harris, 'they reckon that Paul de Luca and his little pals have been nicking cars in the North-West and driving them down to London where Garry's team have been chopping them up. I asked him if they had heard rumours that the gang thought de Luca was a grass and he said it would explain why they had not brought in any cars for several weeks. It's all starting to tie together, Matty lad.'

'Too true it is,' said Gallagher, his eyes gleaming. 'Maybe we are looking at a gangland hit.'

'A somewhat melodramatic phrase but effectively, yes.'

'Is that why I am going to London?'

'We, Matty lad, we.'

'But you hate London.'

'I hate Curtis but I still go and see him sometimes. I would gladly leave this one to you but I think we both need to be there. I want Garry Roscoe.'

'Can't they lift him for us?'

'The Met reckon the gang are bringing in a load of cars on Sunday night and thought we might like to take part in the raid.'

'Would we?' said Gallagher, beaming.

'Thought you'd say that,' said Harris and walked across the room to reach down his coat from one of the pegs. 'Right, I'm off to see Ralph Corbett. Time he answered some questions.'

'I'll go with you,' said Gallagher, standing up.

'No, you stay here. I said you'd ring the lad from the car squad and confirm all the details. He reckons you're old mates.' Harris gave a quirky smile. 'He's another southern wide-boy. His number's on the top of the fax.'

'That can wait.'

But the sergeant's words fell on deaf ears because the inspector was already out of the office and striding down the corridor, Scoot at his heels.

* * *

Darkness was already streaking the northern skies as Ralph Corbett started to close up his animal centre. The poor weather had heralded a bad start to the tourist season and it had been another depressingly quiet day with just the two visitors, a timid couple in their fifties from Scotland, who were staying in a local guest house. Corbett had done his best to make them welcome, explaining the background of his rare pig breeds and offering to let them stroke the creatures. The couple had taken one look at the grubby animals and declined the suggestion. On seeing his visitors looking with interest at the bird cages, Corbett had taken one of the peregrine falcons out and flown it on a lure for their benefit, watching in rapt silence as the bird swooped and dived through the sullen skies. Corbett had commented on the bird's elegance but the couple had seemed less impressed. Indeed, all the time he was guiding them round, Corbett was acutely aware of the expressions on their faces as they glanced at the tired straw matting and tumbledown sheds. Corbett caught the woman more than once wrinkling her nose at the acrid smell of animal excrement and, although she had avoided his look, he knew what she was thinking.

It should not have been like that. He knew that. Before the couple arrived, Corbett had started out the day with the best of intentions, determined to clean all the enclosures out by mid-morning but, as so often in recent months, he found himself distracted: Corbett felt guilty about not being honest with Harris on the occasions he had spoken to the inspector about the burglaries. And although Corbett was sure the detective chief inspector had sensed that there was something more to the break-ins, his friend had seemed reluctant to press the point.

Detective Constable Butterfield had been different, though, and Ralph Corbett had noted with rising alarm during their meeting that morning a sense that she was constantly waiting for him to make a mistake. He found the experience unsettling and, after Butterfield left, he had sat in his office staring at the wall for the best part of an hour. The attitude of the young detective had brought home the realisation that 'out here' – the phrase he always used about his life after retirement from the force – he was just another Joe Public. The thought had made him feel helpless. There had been a time, and not so long ago, when he was someone, when a word from Inspector Ralph Corbett meant something, when young officers like Alison Butterfield would have jumped at his every command. Those were the days, Corbett had told himself as he had sat in the office, a rapidly cooling mug of tea on the desk in front of him. Suddenly, he had felt more vulnerable than he had ever felt in his life.

The constable's visit had left him with mixed emotions. Occasionally, as he recalled the interview, he had scowled at the memory of her dismissive attitude but other times he acknowledged that she was just like he was at that age. Keen. Eager. Determined to make a name for herself. If he was honest, he would also have turned up his nose at the thought of a shed break-in when there was a murder on the patch. And, once or twice, he smiled at the recollection of her interest – despite herself – in his prized woolly sheep, by far the rarest breed at the centre. The thought cheered him a little but it was temporary relief. It was only the arrival of the Scottish couple just before noon that forced him to turn on his public face.

Now they had gone – seeking a teashop in Levton Bridge – and he was busying himself around the centre.

From time to time, as the rain clouds and the late afternoon darkness closed in, he glanced over to the tempting lights in the windows of his house, knowing that his wife was bustling around the kitchen preparing their dinner. But each time he found himself taking a step towards home, he told himself sternly that he still had work to do and redoubled his efforts. Glancing up at the darkening sky, he had walked over to the office to switch on the yard lights before returning to his task.

After a while, he became totally engrossed, constantly talking to the pigs as he settled them down for the night and apologised for neglecting them earlier. As they nuzzled up against him, Corbett felt his turmoil easing and relaxed slightly. This was where he was happiest: you knew where you were with animals, people were far too complicated. It was where he and Jack Harris connected. Eventually, Corbett found himself down the far end of the centre and preparing for his final task of the day, tidying up the tools that had been disturbed during a break-in the previous night. So engrossed had he become in his work that he did not hear the soft footfall on the path behind him as a shadowy figure made its way quietly past the enclosures. Corbett did not know anyone was there until the scraping noise of shoe on ground a few feet away alerted him.

Chapter eight

After leaving the police station, Jack Harris stopped off briefly at the small park on the edge of the town to take Scoot for a walk. The inspector strolled round the park, tutting at the vandalised play equipment that he glimpsed through the dim light afforded by nearby street lamps. There were the occasional sounds of urban life, the slam of a car door, a voice, but for most of the time he was able to enjoy the silence. Leaving Scoot to explore, DCI stared up at the shadowy shapes of the hills. Standing there in the half-light, he felt a sense of desolation, a feeling that the peace had been violated. And that mattered. For Jack Harris, that was important; the hills were his sanctuary, the only place where he found himself at ease with the world, and the idea that someone had disturbed that angered him. It had transformed the death of Paul de Luca into something deeply personal. Harris felt his right fist clenching and took deep breaths to calm himself down, just like he had been taught.

'Pull yourself together, you daft bastard,' he murmured then glanced round to see Scoot approaching down one of the paths. 'Come on, boy. Let's go see Ralph.'

As he turned to go, he saw a figure picking its way across the park towards him. Harris stiffened for a moment then relaxed when he realised that it was the vicar, out walking his own dog.

'I thought I might find you here,' said the Reverend Jameson, a white-haired man. 'Saw the Land Rover parked on the roadside.'

'Taking Scoot for a walk,' said Harris. The vicar's presence was not a surprise, he often saw him on their evening visits and the church was only a few hundred yards away – looking through the darkness now he could see the looming shapes of its gravestones. 'How goes it?'

The vicar did not reply and something about the clergyman's demeanour put Harris on his guard.

'What's the problem, Douglas?' asked the inspector.

Jameson looked uncomfortable.

'Come on, spit it out,' said Harris.

'I'm hearing things,' said the vicar uneasily.

'That'll be the Lord speaking to you.'

Jameson did not reply.

'Ok,' said Harris, 'what things? As if I didn't know.'

'That you're re-opening the investigation into Jimmy Roscoe's disappearance.'

'That's putting it a bit strongly,' said Harris. 'And how come you know about this anyway?'

'People talk. You know that, Jack. One of Edith Roscoe's neighbours said your sergeant had been to see her.'

'And do I take that same someone asked you to suggest that we drop the inquiry?' asked Harris. 'Barry Ramsden perhaps?'

Jameson shook his head vigorously.

'God, no, Jack. And even if he had, I would have declined, you know that. It's none of my business.' The vicar looked at him unhappily. 'It's just that something like this, coupled with the death of Paul de Luca – it frightens people. You know what they are like up here, Jack. I've already had a couple of the old dears on to me. They're not used to this sort of thing. I mean, re-opening the inquiry into Jimmy's disappearance can only do harm. Edith is an old woman and not in the best of health and raising her hopes like this might…'

'You're right,' said Harris, turning to leave the park. 'It is none of your business.'

* * *

'Who found him?' asked Harris grimly, glancing at Butterfield as they stood amid the evening chill of the smallholding.

He had been surprised to find the constable already at the rare breeds centre when he got out of the Land Rover.

'Maureen,' said the constable. 'Called him in for his tea but he didn't show. She found him lying over there.'

Butterfield gestured down the path to the shed, the door to which still stood open, the tools scattered as they had been when she had visited that morning. Somehow, it seemed a long time ago. The constable noticed that the tools did not appear to have been tidied up. She frowned; what on earth had Ralph Corbett been doing since her departure?

'And where is Maureen now?' asked the inspector, glancing over to the house, which was now in darkness. 'Hospital?'

'Yes. Her sister is coming over from Dalby to keep an eye on this place.'

'Any word on Ralph's condition?'

'They've admitted him. He's got a nasty head wound.' She pointed towards the shed. 'There's a lot of blood on the path and some more on the wall.'

'Any chance it was accidental?'

'About as accidental as Paul de Luca.'

Harris stared moodily into the shadows thrown by the yard lights.

'This place is too much for him,' he said, surveying the dilapidated enclosures. 'I keep telling him he should get

95

someone in to help but he won't listen. He can be a stubborn man, can Ralph Corbett.'

Pot and kettle, thought Butterfield, as she wondered when to broach her theory that the break-ins at Corbett's property had something to do with the death of Paul de Luca. Having been brushed aside twice by the inspector earlier in the day, she had spent the afternoon fruitlessly trying to raise the DCI on the mobile to discuss the matter. She and everyone else. Whenever she had seen Curtis, he had looked increasingly angry.

Butterfield knew that she could have told Matty Gallagher her discovery about Ralph Corbett's secret fears but the constable wanted to tell Harris herself: it would be her way of getting involved in her first murder inquiry. However, when the constable returned from Roxham towards late afternoon, having dropped Robert de Luca off back outside the police station, she had found that Matty Gallagher had beaten her to it and that the DCI's office door was closed. And the golden rule was that no one interrupted him when that happened.

The phone call from Control, passing on Maureen Corbett's message about her husband, had arrived as the constable was sitting in the CID office, wondering whether or not to barge into the inspector's office anyway. She knew that now, standing amid Ralph Corbett's enclosures, was the time to raise her concerns. However, something in the inspector's distracted manner caused her to hesitate. Jack Harris could be infuriating at times, she thought, as she watched him walk down the path towards the shed before he stopped to lean on a low wall and gaze at the pigs. Northern men, she thought bleakly. But no, that was wrong: the waters ran deeper with Jack Harris. As she watched, something jerked the chief inspector from his reverie and his eyes widened.

'What the hell is that?' he exclaimed, pointing to a grubby creature snuffling around in the mud.

'Surprised you don't know,' said Butterfield slyly. 'You're the wildlife expert.'

Harris chuckled: he could see the humour in the situation and the comment seemed to relax him slightly.

'Go on then,' said the inspector with a rueful grin. 'What is it?'

'It's a Curly Coated Mangalitza,' said the constable proudly. 'It can trace its heritage back to Lincolnshire. They went extinct over here but you can still get them in eastern Europe – we exported them out there and some UK breeders are trying to build the numbers up again so they can be reintroduced. Seems that Ralph is one of them. He's not a bad old stick when you get to know him.'

'I have heard Ralph Corbett called some things in my time but never that.'

Now, thought Butterfield, now is the time.

'You know earlier today, when I tried to tell you something?' she said.

'Yeah, sorry about that.' He looked genuinely apologetic. 'I've been in the middle of the de Luca thing and I had the phone switched off in case it was Curtis banging on about the lawyers.'

'I heard you're keeping Rawmarsh and Hopson in for another night.'

'Yeah, but I'm pushing my luck, I really am, and I'll have to make a decision in the morning. Curtis will explode if I don't.'

'Does that mean you will be seeing the delectable Ms Reynolds again?'

Harris looked at her sharply. 'Meaning?'

'Nothing.'

'So, what was it you wanted to tell me?' said Harris gruffly, acutely conscious of the young constable's searching gaze.

'Something Ralph Corbett said.' Butterfield was serious again. 'One of his collars when he worked in Merseyside was Paul de Luca.'

'Really?'

'Something about a gang carrying out armed robberies on post offices in the mid-eighties. Paul de Luca supplied the getaway cars for a couple of the jobs. All stolen, of course.'

'Yeah, he got a suspended sentence for it but Ralph Corbett's name is not mentioned in the report. Are you sure you're right about this?' asked Harris.

'Ralph reckons some DS claimed all the credit. He seemed pretty bitter about it.'

'He's bitter about everything. So what happened?'

'He was one of the uniforms when CID raided the gang's headquarters, a garage on an industrial estate. Ralph arrested de Luca as he was trying to climb out of a back window.'

'I wonder why he never told me any of this before,' said Harris.

'He said he knew we would be checking de Luca's background and would be bound to stumble across it, so he wanted to be up front with us. Easier that way, he said. Said murders bring all sorts of things out of the woodwork.'

'They certainly do,' nodded Harris. 'Matty has just been having a go at me for not telling him that I went to school with Paul de Luca.'

'Robert mentioned that as well. Why didn't you say anything?'

It struck her that it was perhaps too direct a question to ask of her boss, especially coming from a lowly constable, but Harris did not seem to be offended. Instead, he considered the comment for a few moments, idly running a finger over the top of the wall then flicking off a piece of moss sticking to a fingernail.

'I guess,' he said at length, 'because I have tried to forget those days.'

'Guv?'

Harris started walking back towards the shed, followed by the constable.

'You talked about things coming out of the woodwork,' said Harris, as she caught him up. 'Well, I guess it will come out soon enough, especially now we are looking at Garry Roscoe.'

He stopped walking and turned to face her. In the half-light, it was difficult for the constable to see his eyes or determine whether or not he was upset. Certainly, when he spoke his voice was quieter than normal.

'It's about the paths we choose,' he said. 'Easy to take the wrong one.'

Butterfield said nothing, waiting for him to continue.

'You ever heard people say that it's a fine line between us and the villains?' he asked.

She nodded.

'Well, you're looking at proof of that. There was a time when I could have gone the wrong side of the line.'

Again she said nothing.

'I hated school,' said Harris. 'I wasn't the brightest and I ended up falling in with a group of lads who were trouble. I was trouble as well, mind. The smaller kids were frightened of us. We used to nick their dinner money – did them over if they refused.'

Harris shook his head at the memory.

'Pretty appalling behaviour,' he said. 'And I'm not proud of it.'

'I take it Paul de Luca was part of your gang?' asked Butterfield, taken aback by the revelation.

'Oh, aye. Him and the Roscoes,' and Harris shook his head again. 'Garry was a nasty piece of work, even then. Jimmy was not so bad, mind. He had this vacant look, always smiling stupidly, like he didn't quite understand what was happening around him. Took it into his adult life as well; that's why he got caught up in car crime. Didn't have the wit to say no.'

Butterfield nodded, she had heard Gallagher talking about the Roscoe case earlier in the day.

'Anyway,' continued Harris, walking towards the shed and peering at the blood smeared on the pig enclosure wall. 'Boy, he did crack his head, didn't he?'

Butterfield nodded but again said nothing, waiting for the inspector to resume his story.

'Where was I?' asked Harris. 'Oh, aye, well we were forever getting into trouble, and it carried on when we went to comprehensive down at Howsham. Only this time, it was more serious, bunking off to go shoplifting, daft acts of vandalism, breaking into cars, couple of robberies, taking kids' bikes, that sort of thing. One morning, Garry turned up to school with this knife. Got himself expelled before he could do anyone any harm. Then one day…'

His voice tailed off and he stared into the middle-distance for a few moments.

'Guv?' asked Butterfield, 'are you alright?'

'Yeah,' he said quietly. 'It's just not something I have ever really talked about. One day, we were in Howsham town centre, bunking off like we always did on a Thursday. It was early afternoon and Garry tried to snatch this old woman's bag. Emily Carlisle, they called her. She was coming out of the Post Office after picking up her pension money. Garry knocked her over and she broke her hip. I can still hear the sound of it snapping.'

The inspector shuddered at the memory.

'Three weeks later, she was dead,' he said softly. 'Never left hospital.'

'Jesus,' breathed Butterfield.

'I still see that woman's face,' said Harris. 'Staring up from the pavement at us. She looked so shocked. She'd done nothing to hurt anyone and she did not deserve that. And I stood by and let it happen.'

He looked at the ground, almost as if he could no longer meet the constable's gaze.

'What happened then?' asked Butterfield after a few moments.

'Her family went to the police, demanding that Garry be prosecuted for manslaughter. We were all questioned – I was terrified, never been in an interview room. Anyhow, the police said they did not have enough to go with it and took Garry to juvenile court for the bag snatch instead. He got three months in juvy. Not that it changed anything. It was like he was proud of what he had done when he came out. Paul de Luca was really impressed by it.'

'And you? What happened to you?'

'Got off with a warning.'

'And did it change anything for you?' asked Butterfield.

'Oh, it changed me alright,' nodded Harris and allowed himself a slight smile. 'That and the thrashing my dad gave me. He was livid but it was more than that – I think he was ashamed.'

Harris closed his eyes for a moment.

'That's a terrible thing to have to say,' he continued. 'That your dad is ashamed of you. My old fella didn't deserve that. When I left school that summer, he took me to sign up for the Army. Said it would sort me out. Tough love, he called it. I kicked up a fuss at first but it turned out to be the best thing he ever did, God bless him. Sometimes you forget how much you owe your father.'

Butterfield was silent for a moment: her thoughts turned to the stormy relationship with her own father. Perhaps, she thought, the time had come to build some bridges. She glanced over at the inspector: the constable felt privileged that Jack Harris had chosen her to unburden himself, to offer a glimpse of what lay behind the barriers which he placed between himself and those around him. But she also felt uncomfortable, like she was witnessing something she was not supposed to see. Now, story at an end, the inspector took a last look at Ralph Corbett's blood smeared on the sty wall.

'What are you thinking, Constable?' he asked.

'I don't know what to think, guv.'

'Well, let's start with Ralph Corbett, shall we?' said the inspector, as if concentrating on police business would banish the intimacy on the moments that had gone before. 'What do you think about what has been happening here?'

'I think,' said Butterfield, trying to sound as casual as possible, but suddenly feeling very hot, 'that what happened here has to be part of the de Luca murder inquiry. I know Ralph's a friend but maybe he knows more than he is letting on.'

Butterfield watched uncertainly as the inspector walked slowly down the path. She knew that the two men had been friends for many years. She waited for the explosion but it did not come.

'Maybe you're right,' said Harris, reaching down over the wall to scratch the snout of a pig that had ambled over to nuzzle him. 'Sorry, pal, I haven't got anything for you.'

He turned to look at her.

'So, Constable, if we assume that Ralph is somehow tied up with this, do we assume that the break-ins are also linked to what happened here tonight? Some kind of campaign of intimidation?'

'Got to be a real possibility, guv, although at first I thought the other ones were down to kids.'

'Could still be. From what I hear, Ralph fell out with some of the teenagers in town a few weeks ago. They were standing where he wanted to park in the market place and he almost ran one of them over. The kids reckon it was deliberate. There was a bit of a scene and words have been exchanged with a couple of the dads several times since.' Harris gave a dry laugh before continuing. 'Perhaps I should take more care choosing my friends, I'm not doing very well at the moment.'

'Guv?'

'Matty is still convinced that Geordie Carroll is mixed up in the de Luca thing somehow. Crime of passion, protecting the birds and all that.'

'Oh, come on, guv,' said Butterfield, 'do you really think anyone would do that just for the eagles?'

'Why not?' said Harris. 'I would.'

In that moment, surveying the inspector's hooded features amid the dancing shadows, and once more unable to see his eyes, the constable was struck once again at how little she – how little any of them – knew Jack Harris. She followed the inspector out of the smallholding.

* * *

An hour and a half later, they were at Roxham Hospital and walking up the stairs to the fourth-floor ward where Ralph Corbett was recovering. It was the inspector's idea that they take the stairs. On the way up, Harris said nothing, continuing the uneasy silence that had persisted in the Land Rover on the drive down the valley. Butterfield surmised that it reflected the chief inspector's concern that he had revealed too much of himself to her. When they reached the ward, Butterfield starting to blow from her exertions, a blonde nurse in her early thirties approached them, carrying a sheaf of files. Her face broke into a smile when she saw the officers.

'Hello, Jack,' she said.

'Julie Marr as I live and breathe,' said Harris affably. 'Which reminds me, I forgot to ask your lad – how was your pizza last night?'

'Oh, we really pushed the boat out,' said Matty Gallagher's wife. 'Had olives on them and get this, Jack, there were black ones and *green* ones. I mean, have you ever heard of such a thing? It's all the rage in London, apparently.'

Harris chuckled, taking the gentle ribbing in good part, and Julie grinned before glancing at Butterfield.

'Two of you,' she said, 'must be something important.'

'Ralph Corbett,' said the constable.

'Nasty one,' nodded Julie, gesturing down the corridor. 'Room eight, second one on the left. His wife is with him.'

When the officers walked into the room, Corbett was sitting up, his head swathed in bandages and his right eye already swollen and blackened. Maureen, a plump woman with a luxuriant head of dark curls despite her years, was sitting next to him and holding his hand.

'How are you feeling?' asked the chief inspector.

'Like I've gone fifteen rounds with Joe Frazier,' said Corbett weakly.

'You got lucky,' said the chief inspector, dragging up a chair and sitting down.

'Yeah, I feel lucky,' said Corbett ruefully, humour forcing its way fleetingly through the pain.

'Going to tell us what happened?'

'Not sure I know really,' said Corbett, shifting slightly on the bed and wincing with the pain. 'It's all a bit of a blank. I was cleaning up, I think.'

'And?'

Corbett paused, as if trying to drag the memory out from his mind then glanced at Butterfield, who was leaning against the wall.

'Hello, pet,' he said.

'Hello, Ralph.'

'So, what happened?' asked Harris.

'Someone came in,' said Corbett, returning his attention to the inspector. 'Yes, someone came in. Walked down one of the paths. He was very quiet. I didn't hear him until he was a few paces behind me.'

'Did you recognise him?'

Corbett shook his head and winced at the pain.

'Remind me not to do that again,' he said, shooting Butterfield a half-smile.

'Can you remember what this man looked like?' she asked.

'Not really. I only got a quick look and it was pretty dark,' said Corbett. 'I spent the best part of thirty years telling witnesses how important details were and the moment I become a victim, I turn out to be bloody useless.'

'Don't worry,' said Harris, reaching across the bed to pat Corbett's hand. 'Just do what you can.'

Corbett nodded and momentarily closed his eyes.

'Can't this wait?' asked Maureen, eyeing her husband with concern.

'You know the score,' said Harris, 'we need as much as we can now.'

She nodded unhappily and the detectives gave Corbett chance to recover his composure. Butterfield was still marvelling at the gentle way in which the inspector had comforted his friend a few moments before. She was seeing another side to Jack Harris. Corbett opened his eyes again. For a moment or two, it looked as if he was not quite sure where he was and he looked around him with a confused expression on his face, then at the detectives. Recognition flickered across his face.

'The doctor says he is concussed,' explained Maureen. 'Ralph, they want to know what happened next.'

'I remember him raising his arm,' said Corbett, as if recalling the incident was a great effort. 'And something else. Yes, he said something. "Hello, Ralph." Yes, that's it. "Hello, Ralph," that's what he said. Next thing I knew, Maureen was standing over me. I guess he struck me.'

'He definitely called you Ralph?' said Harris.

Corbett gave a slight nod of the head.

'So he must have known you,' said the inspector. 'Was it one of the teenagers you pissed off in the marketplace the other week?'

'No, definitely not. This guy was older. Forties, something like that.'

'Could still have been one of their dads, though,' said Harris.

'I don't think it was anything to do with that,' Corbett hesitated.

'So what was it to do with, Ralph?' asked Harris.

'I can't.' Corbett's voice was little more than a croak.

The detectives surveyed him for a moment, struck by the sudden transformation in him. In the low light of the hospital room, Ralph Corbett looked like a ninety-year-old and, like earlier in the day, Butterfield was struck by the fear in his eyes. Corbett noticed their concerned looks and glanced over at Maureen.

'Come on, Ralph,' she said earnestly. 'We can't live with this any longer. Tell them.'

'I can't,' said Corbett quietly. 'They'll kill me.'

'They almost did,' she said.

Instinctively, Corbett reached up to touch his bandage.

'Ralph,' said Harris, 'I've had a long enough day as it is without you playing silly games.'

Corbett hesitated again then glanced over at Maureen.

'Ok,' he said and he looked at Butterfield. 'You know I said I arrested de Luca once?'

She nodded.

'Well, I had meant to tell you the whole truth but got cold feet. That stuff about me arresting de Luca was the only thing I could think of on the spur of the moment.'

'And what is the whole truth?' asked Harris.

'It started four weeks ago. I was walking the dog over by Dead Hill – on the path to Hellens Wood. You'll know it, Hawk.'

Harris nodded, he and Scoot had walked it many times. It was one of their favourite routes.

'That's when I saw him,' said Corbett. 'Recognised him immediately.'

'Who?' asked the inspector. 'Who did you see, Ralph?'

'Garry Roscoe.'

'Are you sure?'

'Yeah, I'm sure,' said Corbett, a new firmness in his voice. 'Don't look like that, Hawk, I've not lost my marbles. I know what I saw. I recognised him from the scar on his cheek.'

Harris nodded – he remembered how Garry Roscoe sustained the injury, falling and hitting his head against a wall during a fight with Paul de Luca in the playground. The inspector remembered how Garry had refused to cry despite the blood pouring down his cheek and how he had carried the scar like a trophy of war afterwards. And he remembered how Paul de Luca had been envious of the adulation which it brought. The two boys' rivalry was never far below the surface.

'How come you knew what he looked like?' asked Butterfield.

'I nicked him once,' said Corbett with a slight smile. 'I've nicked them all in my time. You won't know this, Constable, but before I went to Merseyside, I was at Levton Bridge. I lifted Garry in the act of stealing lead from a church roof.'

'Sounds like his kind of scam,' said Harris.

'He got three months,' continued Ralph. 'I'll never forget the look he gave me when they took him down. Said he'd come for me one day.'

'Yes, but they all say that,' replied the inspector.

'I know that but this time,' Corbett lowered his voice, 'this time it sounded like he meant it. He's a psycho, you know that, Hawk.'

The inspector nodded.

'So, what was Garry doing when you saw him this time?' asked Butterfield.

'I'm not really sure. He was looking over towards the old quarry, the one where de Luca's body was found.'

'And did he see you?' asked the inspector.

'Yeah, came after me,' and Corbett shuddered at the memory. 'Chased me across the moors. I thought he was going to kill me, Hawk, I really did. He was off his head.'

His voice tailed off as he re-lived the memory.

'I tell you, Hawk, I faced down a thousand villains in my time in the force and not once... not once... was I ever scared. But this time...' He closed his eyes.

'Did he recognise you?' asked Harris.

'He knew who I was alright. Said he knew where I lived. Said that if I ever breathed a word about this to you, he would... he would, well, you know. Maureen and all that. She's not been well and...' Corbett's voice tailed off, tears starting in his eyes.

Maureen reached out to hold his hand and he shot her a grateful look.

'So he threatened you directly?' said Harris.

'Said he would torch the place then he'd come after Maureen. I tell you, I haven't slept properly since it happened. Every noise in the night and I've been up.'

'He's been a bag of nerves,' said Maureen.

'And was Garry the one who attacked you tonight?' asked the inspector.

'I just don't know,' said Corbett, frustration clear in his voice. 'Like I said, it was dark and I didn't really get a good look at him. Maybe it was but I couldn't say for certain. I'm sorry, I really am.'

'Why the hell didn't you mention any of this before?' exclaimed the exasperated inspector. 'I mean, all the years we've known each other.'

'I was scared, Hawk.' Corbett lost his battle with the emotion and started to sob. 'Can you believe that, Hawk. Me, scared? Jesus, there was a time when I'd have had toe-rags like him for breakfast. But now...'

He closed his eyes and for a few moments the only sound was the sobs wracking his body. Maureen seemed close to tears as well.

'Ok, ok,' said Harris softly. 'Don't get yourself too distressed.'

Corbett nodded gratefully as Butterfield handed him a paper tissue.

'I take it,' said Harris, once the tears had subsided, 'that you reckon the break-ins were his way of warning you off?'

'I guess so,' said Corbett, voice a little firmer as he looked at his friend. 'What are you thinking?'

'I am thinking that Garry was checking out the quarry as somewhere to kill de Luca.'

'I should have come to you straight off,' said Corbett, looking down at his hands and not meeting the inspector's gaze. 'Stupid, absolutely stupid.'

Noticing Corbett's eyes growing heavy once more, the inspector nodded at Butterfield and stood up.

'You get some rest, Ralph,' he said. 'We'll come back when you are feeling better.'

But Corbett did not answer. He was drifting into sleep. The detectives accompanied Maureen out into the corridor.

'He's been in a terrible state,' she said in a low voice. 'I kept telling him that he should come to you but you know what he's like when he makes up his mind.'

'I do,' said Harris, and reached out to touch her shoulder lightly. 'Let me you know if you need anything.'

After leaving the hospital, Harris and Butterfield headed back to the police station and walked into the CID room to find Matty Gallagher and Robbie Graham sharing a cup of coffee.

'Haven't you got homes to go to?' asked Harris.

'Yeah, we're off,' said Gallagher. 'Julie's at work anyway.'

'We've just seen her,' nodded Harris. 'She was there when we went to see Corbett.'

'How is he?'

'In a bad way,' said Harris, slumping wearily into a chair. 'But he's put Garry Roscoe in the frame for de Luca's murder. We need to find out if Roscoe was working with Rawmarsh and Hopson. I take it you interviewed them again?'

'Yeah, just finished but neither of them have changed their story,' said the sergeant. 'Hadleigh was worse than ever. God, he's an irritating little tit.'

'He is indeed,' chuckled Harris, then glanced over at Robbie Graham. 'Nothing from the background checks?'

'Sorry, guv,' said Graham. 'I've put loads of calls in but no one has come up with anything. Gaynor has been on from Merseyside and they have pulled in a few of Rawmarsh's associates for her but no one has said anything much. And Hopson is as clear as they come.'

Harris sighed and closed his eyes.

'Perhaps,' said Gallagher tentatively, 'they are actually innocent.'

Harris snapped his eyes open again and Gallagher wondered if he had overstepped the mark.

'Maybe you're right,' said the inspector, 'but I don't want to give it up that easily. We'll have another go at them in the morning. If nothing comes of that, we'll let them go. Curtis will implode if we don't.'

'He's never been off the phone,' nodded Gallagher.

'I'll bet,' said Harris, walking over to the windowsill and reaching down to test the warmth of the kettle. 'Top up?'

The detectives nodded and, clutching the kettle, Harris walked out of the office to see Ella Reynolds approaching along the corridor.

'Good evening,' she said, coming to stand so close that the inspector could smell her perfume again.

'Is it?' said the inspector sourly.

'Come on, Jack, time to let it go,' said Reynolds, flashing a smile at him. 'Look, we're both off-duty now. Do you want to grab a drink somewhere?'

The question took Harris by surprise and he looked at her for a few moments, trying to recover his composure.

'Did you just say what I thought you said?'

'I know it's a bit of a drive but I took a taxi down into Roxham last night and found a nice little wine bar. Opens late as well.'

'You took a taxi from here?'

'Mr Hopson is a generous client. Well, what about it?'

Harris shook his head. 'Somehow, I don't think it would be appropriate.'

'Have it your way,' she shrugged and walked down the dimly-lit corridor, her heels clicking on the recently polished floor. 'You know where to find me if you change your mind.'

Later that evening, as he sat in his cottage, trying to concentrate on his book and sipping his whisky, Jack Harris could not get the sound of those heels out of his mind.

Chapter nine

The next morning found Jack Harris sitting in his office and staring across the desk at the anxious figure of Davy Garbutt, the retired officer constantly twisting and untwisting his handkerchief as he sat there, his nerves getting the better of him. The inspector perused him for a few moments. Garbutt looked like someone who had grown old before his time, his eyes dark and hooded, his lips drawn back tight. Gone was the twinkle in the eye and the slightly mocking expression that Harris remembered from Garbutt's final couple of years in the force, a look that indicated someone who knew how to play the game. And Garbutt had always played the game – having managed to persuade senior officers that he was suffering from stress, he had successfully invalided himself out of the force. Harris had seen him a few days afterwards, recalling now how healthy Garbutt had looked when he saw him striding across Levton Bridge Market Place. The experience had left the inspector with a sour taste in his mouth that he felt once again now. Was it an act or was this a genuinely worried man? You never knew with Davy Garbutt.

'So, what's this about?' asked the inspector. 'And make it quick, I'm due in court in a few minutes.'

'I haven't been entirely truthful with you.'

'Now, there's a surprise.'

'Don't be like that, Jack. I know I cut a few corners when I was in the job – you have to in a place like this – but I've never lied to you. You know that.'

'So, what brings you here?'

'I'm scared after what happened to Ralph last night.'

'How do you know about that?'

'Maureen rang me last night. You see, I'm terrified that Garry Roscoe will come after me as well.'

'Why would he do that?'

'Because I saw him up at the quarry as well.'

Harris sat forward. 'When?'

'Same time as Ralph.'

'He never mentioned that you were with him.'

'I asked him to keep me out of it.'

'Why?'

'Didn't want to be involved.'

'Have you thought about what we talked about last time?' asked the inspector. 'Are you sure you're not hiding something? Maybe Garry Roscoe was involved in the death of Jimmy Roscoe?'

'I've told you,' said Garbutt, 'whatever happened to him was an accident.'

'But you knew about the fight with Garry?'

'Like I said last time, I didn't even want to get into that. As far as I was concerned, Jimmy Roscoe was just another missing walker.' He gave a slight smile. 'Anything for a quiet life. You know me.'

'Yeah,' nodded Harris. 'I know you.'

* * *

'This is an absolutely travesty!' exclaimed William Hadleigh furiously as he stalked out of Levton Bridge Magistrates' Court, glancing over at Ella Reynolds as he did so. 'An absolute travesty!'

It was shortly after ten and Hadleigh was speaking while glowering at the retreating backs of Jack Harris and Matty Gallagher as the detectives strode down the busy corridor of the Victorian courthouse, pushing their way between the throng of defendants and witnesses, ignoring the resentful looks they received from some of the defendants. Between them, the two officers had arrested most of them at one time or another. Having also ignored Hadleigh's protests, the detectives paused to have a word with a group of reporters who had scuttled out of the courtroom at the same time.

It had been a ten-minute hearing in which the magistrates had granted the police more time to question Eddy Rawmarsh and Gerald Hopson about the death of Paul de Luca, the chairman of the bench making clear that he thought little of William Hadleigh's shrill comments but showing much more respect to the calm way in which Ella Reynolds presented the case on the part of Gerald Hopson. Respect or not, after retiring to discuss the arguments for little more than two minutes, the magistrates returned and granted police the additional time. Harris thanked him and the detectives left the court immediately, brushing past the blustering Hadleigh. Having completed his conversation with the reporters, Jack Harris patted one of them on the shoulder and started walking once more towards the door which led out into the marketplace.

'Did you hear me!' shouted Hadleigh down the corridor. 'This is a fit-up! You lied your head off in there, Harris!'

The inspector paused in mid-step and Matty Gallagher glanced at him – he had seen men flattened for less. Noticing Harris start to turn, the sergeant held out a restraining arm.

'Leave it,' he hissed. 'He's only trying to wind you up.'

Harris nodded and reached for the door handle.

'Bunch of in-breds,' said Hadleigh loudly.

Harris turned and looked hard at the lawyer, who took a step backwards and glanced at Ella Reynolds for support. She shrugged. Sort your own problems out, her look said. The inspector walked purposefully back towards the solicitors. Gallagher followed in his wake, noticing with alarm that the inspector's right fist was bunched.

'What did you say?' asked Harris through gritted teeth, pressing his face to within inches of the lawyer.

'I think,' said Ella Reynolds, with her usual calm as she stepped in between them, 'that what my colleague was attempting to suggest, albeit in unfortunate terminology, was that we have grave reservations about the way this case has been handled right from the start. Corners have, shall we say, been cut.'

'The magistrates seem to disagree,' said Harris.

'Yeah, but you all know each other up here,' snorted Hadleigh, outrage overcoming fear. 'The chairman is probably related to…'

He got no further because the inspector snapped out an arm and slammed the startled lawyer against the wall.

'I have had enough of your crap!' he snarled, exerting pressure with his forearm so that Hadleigh's feet were off the floor. 'Just sod off and let me do my job!'

Moving quickly, Matty Gallagher stepped forward and placed a hand on the inspector's arm, which was now perilously close to the lawyer's windpipe. Indeed, Hadleigh's face had started to go red as he began to choke. Harris turned to look at his sergeant, fire in his eyes. For a second, the sergeant wondered if his colleague would turn his fury on him – such thoughts were never far away when you worked with Jack Harris – but to his relief, the inspector regained control, gave a slight nod and lowered his arm. Hadleigh crashed onto his knees to grovel on the floor, coughing and spluttering as he clutched his throat.

'Just keep him out of my way!' snapped Harris, glaring at Ella Reynolds.

She opened her mouth as if to say something but thought better of it and instead knelt down to tend to her distressed colleague. Shooting a final baleful look at the wide-eyed people in the corridor, Harris wrenched open the door and stalked into the marketplace.

'I think,' said Gallagher, as the door slammed behind the inspector, causing the building's windows to rattle, 'that might just be a good idea.'

The sergeant looked down at Hadleigh.

'After all,' he said, winking at the lawyer, 'Jack Harris is a trained killer, you know. Ooh, I could tell you some stories. Still, it saves on the paperwork, I suppose.'

Fear flickered across the solicitor's face and, grinning broadly, Gallagher followed the chief inspector out into the bright morning sunshine to find a furious Jack Harris embroiled in a dispute with parish council chairman Barry Ramsden.

'Marvellous,' sighed Gallagher.

Harris jabbed a finger at Ramsden, who was backing away, alarm in his eyes.

'Just get off my back, Barry!' snarled Harris, who shot him a final glare and marched away in the direction of the police station.

'What was that about?' asked Gallagher, walking over to the ashen-faced councillor.

'He just went for me,' said Ramsden.

'For why?'

'All I asked him was when he was going to charge Rawmarsh and Hopson.'

'Bad move,' said Gallagher with a shake of the head and starting to walk down the street after the inspector. 'Bad move.'

As the sergeant turned the corner, he saw Geordie Carroll and Curtis standing at the top of the police station steps. Carroll was gesticulating at the harassed superintendent, who was trying to strike a placatory tone. Guessing what it was about, Gallagher took shelter behind a couple of parked cars, hoping that Carroll would not see him. The ploy failed and, Curtis having gone back into the building, Carroll marched down the stairs, spied the sergeant and strode towards him.

'I warned you!' said Carroll, eyes flashing in triumph. 'I warned you that if you kept asking questions about me, I'd complain to your superintendent.'

'We have to check everyone's story.'

'Poppycock! Making unsupported insinuations, that's what you are doing. Did you really think the other members of the raptor group would not tell me that you had approached them? This amounts to harassment and your superintendent supported me.'

'I'm sure he did,' murmured Gallagher as he watched Carroll stride off in the direction of the market place.

After going a few paces, Carroll turned and pointed at the sergeant.

'Just you keep out of my way!' he said.

'It must be something in the water,' sighed Gallagher and walked into the police station.

* * *

Alison Butterfield sat in the lounge of the terraced house in Manchester and waited for Robert de Luca to bring in the tea. She could hear him bustling round the kitchen. As she waited, she examined the room: with its paintings depicting scenes of Italian life and a framed blue football shirt over the mantelpiece, it suggested someone who still retained strong links with his homeland. Robert came in with a tray and saw her looking at the shirt.

'My prize possession,' he smiled. 'Two years ago – Berlin.'

Butterfield shrugged. 'Don't know much about football,' she said.

'Italy won the World Cup,' he said, setting down the tray and stating to pour the tea. 'Those signatures, they're the team. That one on the left shoulder, that's Fabio Grosso, he scored the winning penalty. And that one on the arm, that's Materazzi. The one that got Zinedine Zidane sent off.'

'I vaguely remember something about that,' nodded Butterfield. 'Didn't he say something about his mother or something?'

'That's the one. The French guy knew what he was doing – you know what Italians are like about their mothers.'

'Were you born in Italy?' asked Butterfield, taking a sip of tea.

'No, we were both born over here. Funny, mind, I still feel Italian, we take the kids over there for holidays but Paul…' His voice tailed off. 'Well, that was Paul.'

'You were very different, I think.'

'Very. Even at school, Paul used to drive my father crazy. I was a bit of a bad lad – so was Hawk, mind – but we were nothing like Paul. When I saw what it was doing to Father, I straightened out. Hawk did the same. That's why he joined the Army. But Paul just kept on getting into trouble. My father never came to terms with that.'

There was a pause as he sipped his tea.

'Why are you here?' he asked.

'DCI Harris wants to know if you can tell us anything about Garry's brother.'

'Jimmy – why would you want to know about him?' de Luca seemed surprised. 'Surely you are not linking him with what happened to Paul?'

'It's just a routine inquiry. You knew him pretty well, I think?'

'I went to school with Jimmy. Funny little lad, he was; then suddenly, in the last year at comprehensive, he started to grow.' De Luca chuckled at the memory. 'It was like Jack and the Beanstalk.'

Butterfield smiled.

'What was he like as a person?' she asked.

'Bit simple, if you ask me. Always had this vacant smile on his face, like he was not all there. That's what got him into trouble. He was a daft lad and people took advantage of him. Garry certainly did.'

'But why him if he was a daft lad?'

'Ah, but he had a gift, Constable. Did you know that Jimmy was good at picking locks?'

Butterfield shook her head.

'That's why Garry wanted him,' said de Luca. 'He was amazing. There wasn't a car Jimmy Roscoe could not get into. My father was forever locking himself out of cars in the garage and Jimmy kept helping him out. It was real gift. I remember the first time he did it – used a coat hanger to get into a Fiat.'

'It's an old police trick,' nodded Butterfield. 'So, what do you know about Jimmy's disappearance?'

'Same as everyone else really. Nothing. After school, we all went our separate ways. The Roscoes ended up getting locked up and I barely even spoke to Paul. He'd got involved with some villains on Merseyside and I figured the less I knew the better.'

There was silence for a few moments.

'Do you have a brother?' asked de Luca.

'No.'

'Well then you can't know what it's like.' His face assumed a sad expression. 'You're really close as kids, fight each other's battles, you against the world, all that kind of stuff but when you grow older something happens. You make your choices and things are never quite the same. It was like that with me and Paul. We became like strangers.'

He lapsed into silence.

'I am sorry,' he said eventually. 'You don't want to hear this. I am not being much help, I am afraid. Do you really think Jimmy's disappearance has something to do with Paul's murder?'

Butterfield shrugged.

'At the moment,' she said, 'I'm not sure we think anything.'

* * *

119

Shortly after 11am, Harris was sitting in his office, staring moodily out of the window and noticing without much surprise that the sun had faded once more and that it had started to rain again. His reverie was disturbed by a knock on the door and Superintendent Curtis entered.

'Now I wonder what you've come about,' said the inspector, eying him warily.

'Where do I start?' said Curtis, closing the door behind him, dragging up a chair and sitting down. 'Assaulting a lawyer, letting your sergeant intimidate Geordie Carroll, abusing the parish council chairman. Do you have any idea what damage this kind of thing can do? I should suspend you. In fact…'

'Spare me the lecture. If you're going to suspend me, just do it.'

'Actually, I'm not.'

'You're not?' said Harris suspiciously.

'No, in fact,' said the superintendent, with the slightest of smiles. 'I'm not sure that even Jesus Christ himself could have resisted the temptation to plant one on William Hadleigh. The man is a pillock of the first water. And as for that half-arse Ramsden…'

Harris looked at him in surprise: he had never seen Philip Curtis exhibit any evidence that he possessed an irreverent side to his nature. That it should surface at such a time as this was even more remarkable. The inspector decided to be conciliatory.

'I lost it and I'm sorry,' he said. 'It won't happen again.'

'I do hope not, because if it does, I will have no alternative but to relieve you of your duties. However, your little wrestling match with Hadleigh is not the main thing I wanted to talk to you about. I hear the court gave you additional time to question Rawmarsh and Hopson.'

'We've got till midnight.'

'Well, in the circumstances I think we should release them now.'

Harris gaped at him. 'What!'

'Ella Reynolds has just had another go at me and I have to say that I agree with her. Why are those men still here, Jack? We've nothing to link them to the death of Paul de Luca.'

'Yes, but…'

'How many times have you interviewed them now?'

'Four, but…'

'And still nothing,' said Curtis. 'Their story has not changed and you have not produced a shred of evidence against them apart from a somewhat dubious eyewitness and a lot of idle gossip. Come on, Jack, just admit you've got it wrong.'

'Not necessarily. There may be a link with Merseyside,' said the inspector vaguely. 'And Rawmarsh is from Liverpool.'

'So is my aunt, do you want to pull her in for questioning?' There was an edge to the superintendent's voice. 'Look, I know you detest Eddy Rawmarsh – he's not exactly my favourite person – but don't let that cloud your judgement. Release them or charge them.'

'But the chairman of the bench said…'

'Come on. Everyone knows you and William Gatenby go way back. For God's sake, from what I hear, you were drinking together in The Black Bull at the weekend.'

'That's hardly a crime,' said Harris sulkily.

'But it does not look very good, particularly when Ella Reynolds is now threatening to take us to the High Court for wrongful arrest of her client.'

'Yes, but can she really do that?'

'I don't want to have to find out and I do hear talk that she has already retained a barrister. Besides, that's not the only reason I want a decision, HQ are already asking why we aren't looking at anyone else for the murder.'

'You know we are.'

'Yes, but from what I hear, your sergeant is gallivanting round trying to make out that Garry killed his brother when it seems more likely that he fell down a mine shaft.'

'But we can also link Garry to Paul de Luca,' said Harris.

'Then if he such a good bet, why are we still holding the others?' and Curtis stood up. 'Like I said, release them or charge them, Jack. It's your choice.'

'It seems,' said the inspector in a cold voice, 'that it isn't.'

'In which case,' said Curtis, walking to the door, 'get them out of my sodding police station and get it done now.'

* * *

Twenty minutes later, the grim-faced inspector and his bemused sergeant were standing in the reception area, watching a smirking Eddy Rawmarsh and a grinning Gerald Hopson preparing to leave the police station. Alongside them was William Hadleigh, unable to conceal his jubilation as he shot triumphant glances at the chief inspector. Harris noted with satisfaction that the lawyer had a red mark on his neck. Alongside Hadleigh stood Ella Reynolds, regarding the scene with a sense of cool detachment.

'I am glad,' she said, walking over to Harris, 'that common sense was allowed to prevail in the end. No hard feelings, I hope. Not that I object to hard feelings.'

'Your clients should not be going anywhere,' said the inspector, 'not if I had my way.'

'And you do like to have your way,' replied Reynolds.

Gallagher glanced at the inspector for any sign that he had picked up the innuendo but Harris remained impassive.

'They still have a lot of questions to answer,' was all he said.

'Well,' said Rawmarsh, wrenching open the door onto the street, 'if you've got any more questions, you'd better ask someone else, Jacky-boy, because I'm out of here and I ain't coming back.'

Hopson gave one of his girlish giggles and followed the Liverpudlian out of the police station and down the steps, both men pausing to appreciate the fresh air. Hadleigh followed them outside, skirting nervously round the glowering inspector, loathe to risk another confrontation with the burly officer. As he went outside, Hadleigh instinctively reached up to rub his neck, which was still sore from the incident in the courthouse. In doing so, he let the door swing back into Ella Reynolds's face.

'Such a charming man,' she murmured.

Jack Harris opened the door for her.

'Thank you,' she said. 'At least someone has some manners around here.'

She extended a gloved hand and Harris shook it. The fingers felt soft and supple through the black leather. He liked the feeling.

'Goodbye, Chief Inspector,' she said. 'Maybe we will meet another time. Perhaps in more pleasant circumstances.'

Harris, who could think of plenty of more pleasant circumstances involving Ella Reynolds, said nothing as he watched her walk down the steps to where a knot of newspaper and radio journalists and couple of television crews had gathered. She moved to stand next to Hadleigh and the released men, reached into her coat pocket and produced a piece of paper.

'I would like to make a brief statement on behalf of Eddy Rawmarsh and Gerald Hopson,' she said as the journalists edged forward.

There was the click of photographers' cameras.

'Both men,' said Reynolds, slipping smoothly into her act, 'feel that they have been unfairly treated by police in Levton Bridge. At no point have detectives presented any firm evidence to link our clients with the unfortunate death of Paul de Luca earlier this week. To that end, we will be instigating proceedings for unlawful arrest and seeking appropriate recompense from the police. We cannot stand by and let innocent men – other innocent people as well, for all we know – be subject to the kind of treatment that our clients have received in this backwater over recent days. It really is like something out of the Wild West up here.'

'Oh, please,' murmured Harris as the reporters scribbled furiously.

Standing at the top of the steps, he had viewed the scene with a grim expression on his face. Gallagher glanced up and noticed Superintendent Curtis watching the events below out of an office window. His expression was equally dark.

'However,' continued Ella Reynolds, 'we are delighted that our clients have finally been released, despite the misguided decision of the court to allow police more time to question them. There are people in this town who need to ask themselves some searching questions about what they allow their police force and their judiciary to do in the name of justice. That is all. Thank you, ladies and gentlemen.'

With that, and waving away questions from the excited journalists, she walked briskly to a waiting taxi, beckoning at Gerald Hopson to join her.

'Like a lapdog,' snorted Harris.

'Surely they're not going all the way back in that,' whispered Gallagher as he saw the taxi driver reach forward to activate the meter. 'It'll cost a fortune.'

'It seems that our Mr Hopson does indeed have deep pockets,' said Harris as the taxi pulled away and the lawyer waved at him through the passenger seat window.

'She seems to have a bit of a thing for you,' said Gallagher tentatively.

'Meaning?' asked Harris sharply.

'London birds like a bit of northern rough.'

The inspector gave his sergeant a sour look. Gallagher wondered whether or not to ask about the previous night but something in the DCI's expression suggested it might be a bad idea so the sergeant returned his attention to Rawmarsh and Hadleigh, who were completing their interview with a television reporter. They walked over to Hadleigh's Jaguar and seconds later the car backed into the road, pulling up at the bottom of the steps. Eddy Rawmarsh wound down the passenger side window and after a glance at the assembled journalists, gave a mocking smile in the detectives' direction.

'Time for us to ride out of this little old Wild West town,' he said, giving the inspector a mock salute. 'Maybe we'll meet up again sometime, *pardner*.'

And with a loud laugh, he wound the window back up and the Jaguar pulled away.

'Sooner than you think, Eddy,' murmured Harris. 'Sooner than you think.'

Then, refusing the journalists' requests for a statement, the chief inspector stalked back into the building. From his first-floor vantage point, Philip Curtis turned back into the room.

Standing at the far end of the road, the man watched the Jaguar leave the police station. Shrinking back into a back alley to avoid being noticed, he allowed himself a slight smile.

'Bye, bye, boys,' he said.

After the two suspects had departed, Harris and his sergeant strolled back through the police station corridors, deep in conversation as they walked into the CID room. As they entered, talk among the six detectives died away. Harris noticed their expectant looks and, standing before them, let his eyes range slowly round the room.

'Am I supposed to say something?' he said. 'Have I missed someone's birthday?'

No one laughed.

'We just want to know where we go now, guv,' said Robbie Graham. 'I mean, now we've let them go.'

'We keep digging for something linking Rawmarsh and Hopson to the murder.'

'But you've released them,' said Graham.

'Correction,' said Harris. 'The super released them, in his infinite wisdom. And just because he let them go does not mean that they are off the hook. We know Garry Roscoe was working with de Luca and that puts Rawmarsh and Hopson in on things as well.'

The inspector noticed Robbie Graham shaking his head.

'Come on, Robbie,' said Harris. 'Share it with us.'

Graham glanced around at the other detectives for support. Butterfield nodded her encouragement but still Graham hesitated.

'Come on, Robbie,' said Harris. 'I won't bite.'

There was still silence.

'Scoot might, though,' added the DCI, nodding at the dog, who was snoozing beside a radiator.

The joke eased the tension for a second.

'Ok,' said Graham, glancing at the other detectives, 'we've been talking among ourselves and we really do not believe that Eddy Rawmarsh is part of this.'

'Is that right?' asked Harris, his voice ominously quiet.

'Yes,' nodded Graham, looking at two officers sitting by the window. 'I mean, you've had Phil and Gaynor down in Liverpool for two days and they've come up with nothing and the rest of us have talked to countless officers in various forces yet no one has come up with a single thing to link either of these guys with the murder.'

'Yet.'

'It's alright you saying that,' replied Graham, growing in confidence, 'but all I'm saying is maybe it was coincidence that they were in the quarry. Wrong place, wrong time. It does happen.'

He looked round the room but none of the other detectives met his eye, unnerved by the inspector's coldness. Matty Gallagher, perched on the corner of a desk behind the chief inspector, closed his eyes momentarily. He'd had words with Robbie Graham before about overstepping the mark. It had been the same with Alison Butterfield. Promising detectives, they may be, the sergeant thought, but they still had to learn how to express their opinions, especially to senior officers, and especially to someone like Jack Harris with his short fuse. The sergeant wondered whether or not to intervene but the constable's next words banished the thought.

'And what's the sarge been doing?' said Graham, glancing at Gallagher. 'Wasting his time on a bloke who took a header down a bleeding mine shaft.'

Gallagher frowned and, deciding he had had enough peace-making for one day, decided that if Robbie Graham could not read the danger signs, if he really wanted to walk into trouble, then that was his lookout. Maybe a dressing-down at the hands of Jack Harris – once experienced, such events were never forgotten – would knock some sense into the young officer, he decided. Mind made up on the matter, the sergeant sat back and enjoyed the show.

'All I'm saying,' replied Graham, confidence starting to drain away under the inspector's wilting stare, 'is that maybe this thing you have against Eddy Rawmarsh may be… well, you know…'

His voice tailed off.

'Let's assume I don't,' said Harris.

Sitting watching the confrontation, Gallagher wondered idly if the constable's cockiness had anything to do with the fact that his father was a DCI at headquarters, and an ambitious one at that, one who wanted to be free of the pen-pushing and craved a divisional CID command of his own. The knowledge had never sat comfortably with Gallagher and he knew that Jack Harris had objected when informed that Robbie would be coming to work at Levton

Bridge. 'Michael Graham's man on the inside,' Harris had said with a derisory snort. Now, Gallagher gave a half-smile and watched Harris as the inspector fixed Robbie Graham with a steely stare.

'Well,' said Harris as the constable hesitated. 'Out with it. Let's assume I don't know what you are talking about. Let's assume I'm some sort of fucking idiot, shall we?'

Gallagher winced and the blood started to drain from Robbie Graham's face.

'Go on,' said Harris, 'tell me how to run this inquiry. Every other bastard seems to want to – the parish council chairman has had a go, some old dear in Chapel Ebton has made a few suggestions and the vicar's chucked in his two-penn'orth, so why should you be any different? Or maybe you want to give your dad a call instead, see what he thinks?'

Gallagher closed his eyes again. Maybe he would have to intervene after all.

'I'm not saying that,' said Graham, growing flustered in the face of inspector's cold anger, 'I'm just saying that your personal antipathy to Eddy Rawmarsh might be… clouding your judgement.'

There was a sharp intake of breath from the other detectives and Gallagher instinctively glanced at the DCI's hands, which were clasped behind his back. He was relieved to see no sign of bunched fists. Instead, Harris walked over to the window and stared down into the street, where the journalists were starting to disperse and a television reporter was recording a piece to camera. Harris could just hear his name being mentioned. After spending a moment or two admiring the attractive young blonde journalist, the inspector turned back to the room.

'Is that it?' he asked quietly.

'Look, don't take it the wrong way, guv,' said Graham uncomfortably, glancing round at the other detectives for support but alarmed to find them still averting their gazes. 'You always say we should challenge the evidence.'

Harris looked out of the window again: the television reporter had finished recording her piece and the crew were starting to pack up their gear. The reporter glanced up and caught his eye. The DCI smiled and she smiled back. Matty Gallagher leaned over to peer through the window as well and caught the girl's gesture. Harris glanced over at the sergeant and winked at him.

* * *

Having stopped at Levton Bridge's only petrol station, William Hadleigh's Jaguar headed through the market place then up the winding, steep hill on the eastern fringes of the town, past the Victorian primary school with its grey slate roof, the tiles glistening with the light rain that had started to fall. Just past the school, the road narrowed briefly, not helped by the cars parked on either side, and although Hadleigh saw the delivery van approaching from the other end, he did not slow down, instead gunning the Jaguar through the gap and forcing the other driver to haul hard on the brakes. Hadleigh grinned at the van driver's foul expression as the Jaguar shot past him.

Within a few moments, the terraced houses petered out and the road took a sharp bend before weaving its way up onto the tops. Although stunning views had opened across the windswept moors, neither of the men seemed to have noticed them as they travelled in silence, Hadleigh concentrating on the road, Eddy Rawmarsh puffing on a cigarette.

Within a quarter of a mile, the road widened and Hadleigh pressed his foot onto the accelerator, smiling as the engine gave a deep-throated roar and the car leapt forward. Soon the speedometer said that they were travelling at seventy-five miles per hour along the straight moorland road. Within five minutes, they approached Drovers' Bend where the road dipped steeply downwards and crossed a little stone bridge beneath which ran a beck.

As Hadleigh approached the bridge, a sheep ran out in front of the vehicle and the lawyer swore and slammed his foot onto the brakes. Nothing happened and the car swerved wildly, one of its wheels striking a rock on the roadside, the impact sending the Jaguar careening back across the road to leave the ground momentarily before ploughing into the base of the bridge. There was dull thud then a smashing of glass followed by a muffled sound as the car burst into flames. No one heard the men's screams as they burned to death.

Chapter ten

'This was a professional job,' said the vehicle examiner, clambering up the muddy bank.

It was late afternoon and the light was fading fast as Gallagher and Harris stood on the road above the bridge and looked down upon the shattered wreckage of William Hadleigh's vehicle. The car, which was still smouldering, had come to rest with its front end buried in the soft soil on the edge of the stream, and with its rear wheels dangling several feet off the ground. The interior had been burned out and the windows had shattered. From their vantage point, the detectives could clearly see the charred remains of Eddy Rawmarsh and his lawyer, both sitting bolt upright in their seats, given no time to react by the suddenness of the crash that had taken their lives. Even to hardened police officers, even to Jack Harris who had detested them both, the sight of the bodies was a difficult one to view.

'What do you mean a professional job?' asked the chief inspector as the vehicle examiner came to stand next to the detectives.

'I mean someone doctored the brakes,' said the examiner, turning up his coat collar against the chill wind now blowing in off the moors.

'Cut them, you mean?' asked Gallagher.

'In simplistic terms, yes, but done very skilfully. I'll know more when we get the car back to the workshop but I reckon the brakes were fixed so that they did not fail immediately.'

'Can you do that?' asked Harris.

'If you know what you are doing,' answered Gallagher before the examiner could open his mouth. 'We had a case like it when I was on the Met's auto crime unit. Car drove round for a day-and-half. The brakes finally went when it was driving down towards a canal. Three teenagers died.'

'There's a real art to it,' added the examiner, looking down at the vehicle and speaking almost as if he admired what had been done. 'Most people who try this sort of thing botch it up because the brakes fail when the victim is only travelling slowly. But whoever did this one…'

And he looked down at the forensics officers picking their way around the vehicle. 'Whoever did this must know cars inside out.'

'Garry Roscoe,' murmured Harris, glancing at his sergeant then back at the crumpled Jaguar. 'I said Eddy Rawmarsh was mixed up in this somewhere, Matty.'

The officers stood for a few moments and watched the vehicle examiner slip-slide his way back down the bank to resume his inspection of the Jaguar.

'Reminds me of Northern Ireland,' said Harris.

'Guv?' Gallagher could not remember the last time he had heard the inspector mention his military days.

'A bomb. Blew up one of our vehicles, killed two of the lads. I was travelling behind them.'

The sergeant waited for Harris to elaborate but he didn't, instead surveying the burned-out Jaguar in silence, lost for a moment in memories of turbulent times on the Falls Road.

'So what do we do now?' asked Gallagher. 'Get the Met to haul Roscoe in now?'

'Can't do that, the Met say they need to get his gang with the stolen cars. If we start asking too many questions about Garry Roscoe now, it might scare him off.'

'Maybe he knows already,' said Gallagher. 'You're always saying everyone knows everyone. Maybe someone has tipped him off.'

'The thought had occurred,' said Harris, rubbing his chin. 'So how's about this for an idea? We create a big fuss, pull in every garage owner in the area, haul in every petty car thief we know about, make a huge noise about things, give the impression that we are pretty sure it's a local job? Get the media circus involved, let them come on some of the raids. They'll love that and there is no way Garry could become suspicious then, even when he heard about it. He'd just assume we were desperate.'

'Good plan.'

'Get it under way then. Get Merseyside and GMP to play along. Then once that is up and running, you and I can slip off to London and bring this nonsense to an end.'

'Even better plan,' said Gallagher.

* * *

Jack Harris stood at the front of Levton Bridge Police Station the following morning and watched as a stream of officers guided a succession of protesting men up the steps. Noticing Gallagher alighting from the passenger door of a patrol car that had just drawn up, the inspector walked down to greet him.

'Who you got?' he asked.

'Shane Wordsworth,' said the sergeant, opening the back door to usher out a wiry little man in his early forties. 'Come on, Shaney boy, out you get.'

'What's this about?' asked Wordsworth resentfully, 'I ain't done nothing wrong.'

'Oh, there's always something,' said Gallagher cheerfully and took him into the station.

Glancing down the street, Harris saw a middle-aged woman walking up the hill toward the police station.

'Gillian,' he said, holding out his arms. 'What can I say?'

'You can say you're a bastard, that you are very, very sorry and it'll never happen again,' said Detective Inspector Gillian Roberts.

'I am sorry, but we don't have something like this very often.'

'Leave you alone for five days and the world collapses,' said Roberts.

It was with great reluctance that Harris had recalled his DI from her holiday: he had always regarded leave as sacrosanct but, once it became clear that he had to go to London with Gallagher, Harris knew he had no options. He knew he needed an experienced hand and they did not come any more experienced than Gillian Roberts. A mother-of-two in her early fifties, she affected a somewhat matronly demeanour but those who had crossed her knew it was just an act. Gillian Roberts was as tough as they came and, crucially for Harris, unflappable in a crisis. She had once said that having two boys meant that everyday police crises simply paled into insignificance: having talked a surly teenager out of his locked bedroom after a row with his girlfriend, truculent villains were nothing. Remembering his own difficult early years and the impact they had on his parents, Harris had nodded when she had made the comment.

Now, Harris looked at her affectionately as she led the way towards the front door. Before she grabbed hold of the handle, another patrol car pulled up behind them and they turned to see Robbie Graham get out of the back with an unsavoury character in tow.

'Who's Boy Wonder got?' asked Roberts.

'Could be anyone,' said Harris, adding with a grin, 'I think he was told to do D to G.'

'You pulling everyone in then?'

'Not the vicar.'

'Why on earth not? Time someone locked him up for his sanctimonious sermons.'

Harris chuckled then wiped the smile from his face as Robbie Graham walked up the steps towards them, studiously avoiding the chief inspector's gaze and scuttling into the station with his man.

'You two had words?' asked Roberts, turning to look at the chief inspector.

'Tried to tell me how to do my job.'

'Ah.'

'Talking of which,' said Harris as there was a shout and he saw Barry Ramsden running up the street. 'Here's chairman of t'committee.'

Roberts gave a low laugh.

'Jack,' said Ramsden, walking up the stairs and approaching Harris respectfully, mindful of their last fractious meeting. 'Glad I caught you, I wanted a word.'

'About what – as if I didn't know?' said the inspector, gesturing for the DI to go inside.

'About this.' Ramsden looked at the police cars parked out of the front of the police station. 'I hear you have brought in a few of the local garage owners.'

'Sorry, I can't tell you anything. This is a major operation, Barry. You know how it is,' and he tapped the side of his nose conspiratorially. 'It's on a need to know basis.'

'Yes, I appreciate that but surely the chairman of the parish council could be taken into your confidence?'

He looked hopefully at Harris. The inspector, for his part, knew what the question was about. Ramsden had always prided himself on knowing everything that was going on in the town, it was a point he never failed to make whenever the opportunity arose. Harris knew that Ramsden would have been embarrassed at being unable to shed light on the police raids when asked by local people.

Taking his time, the inspector gave the impression of being deep in thought.

'Ok, Barry,' he said, lowering his voice, 'you can help us. But this goes nowhere else, right? I have to know I can trust you.'

'You know me, Jack,' Ramsden said, his eyes gleaming.

Harris nodded.

'Ok,' he said. 'I need your support because we're going to have to build an extension to the morgue with all these bodies. Can you help us get planning permission?'

Leaving an open-mouthed Ramsden standing in the street, the inspector turned and walked into the police station with a huge grin on his face.

Chapter eleven

'God, I hate London,' murmured Harris, peering out of the train window.

It was late Sunday afternoon and his mood had grown steadily worse as the train left behind the rolling hills of the Pennines and the towns and cities along the line had grown more numerous. For Jack Harris, leaving Levton Bridge always had the same effect. A man who had grown up in the northern hills, he had always felt their pull wherever in the world he was. When he was away from them, it was as if part of him was missing and during his Army days, he had been at his most comfortable when the regiment was working far away from people, out in the high-skied deserts of Africa and the Middle East or deep in the verdant valleys of the Balkans, places where you could sit at night and hear the silence, just as he had always done at home. That opportunity to work away from the big cities was why he had specialised in special operations and why he had detested the regiment's time in Belfast. Most soldiers had hated Northern Ireland because of the ever-present danger but Jack Harris had hated it simply because there were too many people. It was the same feeling that had driven him to quit his job in the Greater Manchester police force and apply instead for a posting back to Levton Bridge. It was the same feeling that he felt now as the train sped south.

For a while it had looked as if Gallagher would have to make the journey to London on his own, the fallout from the car crash leading to a media frenzy with the police station besieged by excited journalists eager for any shred of new information. There had been community issues to confront as well: Harris had read the statistics, knew that fear of crime was highest in rural areas where there were few offences, knew that even the smallest incident could send the fear rippling out across the hills – so the deaths of Hadleigh and Rawmarsh, coming so soon after that of Paul de Luca, was a major cause for concern. Despite taking the view that assuaging such worries was the superintendent's job, Harris had nevertheless found himself fending off a succession of calls from worried community leaders as the weekend had progressed. Barry Ramsden himself had telephoned on five occasions.

So, dislike of London or not, part of Harris had welcomed the decision to leave the town for a day or two. But now, as the train entered the outer edges of the capital, such feelings had long since been banished. The inspector gazed out at the grey high-rises and the derelict factories, at the litter-strewn wastelands and the graffiti-daubed railway buildings, his expression growing ever darker. The inspector sighed and felt, sharp almost as if it were a pain, a yearning for the moors, to be out walking with Scoot, whom he had reluctantly left with Alison Butterfield. Sitting opposite him, Matty Gallagher watched him gloomily.

A few minutes later, the train pulled into the station and the detectives stepped onto the busy platform and fought their way against the tide of shoppers and day-trippers jostling and scurrying for their trains, barging and bumping their way past the detectives as the officers carved a path through their ranks.

'How can people live like this?' muttered the chief inspector as a large woman collided with him, one of her shopping bags striking his knee and making him wince. 'Everyone in such a bloody hurry?'

Matty Gallagher chuckled at the inspector's discomfort as his own spirits soared. The sergeant was loving every minute of the experience, revelling being back in the city of his birth. This was where Gallagher came alive and now he was, as always, excited by the sounds and the smells, and the sheer feel of London. After spending five months in the inspector's world, the sergeant was relishing the roles being reversed for once. As he walked along the platform, Gallagher constantly looked around, his eyes bright as they devoured every image. He could also just hear over the scampering feet and the PA announcements the hum of traffic and the honking of car horns outside the railway station. The promise of the wider city. Gallagher sighed with pleasure and his face broke into a broad grin when he saw, standing at the end of the platform, a wiry dark-haired man in a black suit.

'Danny Raine,' said Gallagher. 'That DI you talked to on the phone.'

'Another bloody chirpy Cockney,' said Harris sourly as he swerved to avoid a harassed mother dragging two complaining children along the platform. 'Maybe he's got some jellied eels for us. We can stuff them into our boat races as we go up the apples and pears.'

Gallagher laughed out loud: not even the inspector's sour mood could dampen down the sergeant's enthusiasm at being back in the capital and he had determined to enjoy every minute of it. As the detectives reached the end of the platform, Danny Raine stepped forward and extended a hand of welcome.

'Matty Gallagher as I live and breathe,' he said delightedly.

'Danny,' said the sergeant, shaking the hand enthusiastically. 'How the hell are you?'

'All the better for seeing you, matey. And this,' said Raine, turning to the detective chief inspector and extending his hand again, 'must be Jack Harris. I have heard all about you, sir. This is a real privilege, believe me.'

'It is?' said Harris suspiciously as he shook the hand and they started to walk off the platform. 'Why would that be?'

'Why? Because you're a legend, sir.'

Harris stopped walking and eyed the detective inspector dubiously.

'Are you taking the mick?'

'Na,' grinned the DI. 'It's straight up. I saw you give a lecture about peregrine falcons at University College.'

'You did?'

'Yeah, must have been three years ago now. You had a real go at the pigeon fanciers for persecuting the falcons. There was an article in one of their magazines about it afterwards. Called you a "thick plod" as I recall.'

'It did indeed.' Harris chuckled at the memory. 'I've got it on my office wall.'

'He has,' said Gallagher. 'Though why anyone would want something like there up in lights I have no idea.'

'Matty does not understand these things,' said Harris as they pushed their way through the crowds gathering in front of the departure boards. 'I have to say that I am surprised to find that you do, Danny.'

Raine allowed himself a sly look at Gallagher.

'We're not all townies, you know,' he said.

Harris smiled. He was starting to like Danny Raine.

'So how come you are interested in hawks?' he asked as they walked toward the station exit.

'My dad used to keep falcons. He used to fly them on the local heath. He had this one Harris hawk, I remember. Beautiful bird, it was.'

'They call me Hawk, happy for you to do the same,' said Harris, clapping the detective inspector on the shoulder. 'In fact, I insist on it.'

Coming to a halt on the station concourse and watching in bemusement as the two detectives headed out into the busy city streets, deep in conversation, Matty Gallagher raised his eyes to the ceiling.

'Perhaps this wasn't such a good idea,' he murmured.

* * *

Three hours later, it felt like the best idea in the world. With darkness having fallen over the capital, all talk of birds had long been forgotten as Harris and Gallagher walked into the police station briefing room and took their seats among the plainclothes detectives and uniforms preparing for the raid on Garry Roscoe's workshop. As they entered, a few of the officers stood up and walked over to shake Matty Gallagher's hand and he in turn introduced Harris. For his part, the chief inspector noted the respectful way the London officers talked to their northern counterparts and his mind wandered briefly back to Robbie Graham's cocky attitude. Jack Harris found himself warming to his new acquaintances.

Introductions complete, the two detectives sat down again. Jack Harris looked around and experienced a frisson of excitement, of anticipation. He acknowledged that, despite himself, he was enjoying being at the centre of a major operation in the heart of a great city. Sitting in the briefing room in the middle of London, he came to the conclusion that perhaps Curtis was right to distrust his judgement. Noting how the incidents of the past week had invigorated him, the inspector realised just how deep a rut he had slipped into down the years. Filled with a new determination, he leaned over and was about to say something to the sergeant when the door opened and in walked Danny Raine.

'Ladies and gentlemen,' said Raine, making his way to the front of the room. 'Thank you for coming. I think we all know why we are here.'

The DI turned and pointed to a large board behind him, in the middle of which was a photograph of a back-street garage standing half way along a rundown terrace of houses. With its brickwork crumbling and the green paint on the garage door peeling away, it was the sort of place no one would look at twice, the reason the gang had selected it to break up the stolen cars. Fanned out around the photograph were the images of a half a dozen men. Surveying the faces, Matty Gallagher's attention was drawn to one in particular, a sallow, lean-faced, pock-marked character whose nose was bent out of shape like that of a prize-fighter and with that distinctive scar on his cheek. But it was not the legacies of battle that held the sergeant's attention, it was the eyes. He had seen them before and was transported back to the dim little cottage in Chapel Ebton and to that faded school photograph of Jimmy Roscoe.

'Garry,' said Harris, reading the sergeant's thoughts. 'People always reckoned they were twins but Jimmy was a year-and-half older.'

'These men are our targets tonight,' said Raine, pointing at the photographs then tapping the one of Roscoe. 'This guy is our main man. Garry Roscoe. Watch out for him, he's a nasty bit of work. The rest I think most of you know. If not, familiarise yourself with them before you go. We've invested too much time and effort in this operation to balls it up now.'

Raine looked towards Harris.

'Now,' he said, 'I would like to introduce our visitors for those who do not know them. Matty Gallagher, many of you know already: indeed, a few of you will have enjoyed drunken evenings with him. Coming to think of it, knowing Matty Gallagher you probably won't remember.'

There were a few laughs and Gallagher stood up and gave a little bow.

'And I am delighted to say that with him is DCI Jack Harris,' continued Raine after allowing the laughter to subside. 'Some of you will have heard me talking about him. Do you want to say a few words, sir?'

Harris nodded and walked to the front of the room.

'We are also interested in this little lot,' he said, gesturing to the faces on the board, 'because of their links with Paul de Luca. At first we had two other guys in the frame but now we think it's down to Garry Roscoe. We have reliable eyewitness reports that put him in our area at the right time.'

'I know you think he's reliable,' said Raine, 'but we have been watching him for weeks and we are still pretty sure he hasn't left the city. Are your informants sure?'

'They're both ex-job.'

'Who are the other guys you had in the frame?' asked another officer.

'One of them was a Scouser called Eddy Rawmarsh. Does the name ring a bell with anyone?'

The inspector looked round the room and was disappointed to see blank looks from the officers.

'And the other guy?' said someone.

'Chap called Hopson but I can't see him being...'

'Not Gerry Hopson?' said a voice from the back of the room and a plainclothes officer stood up.

Harris nodded. 'You know him?'

'I used to work in Robbery and we'd been after him for years. In fact, we had just started looking at him for laundering cash from a series of jobs carried on big houses in the west end. Nasty stuff, one old guy got his leg broken when he refused to show them where the safe was.'

'Why don't we pull him in?' said Raine, looking at the officer. 'Can you clear it with Robbery?'

'Will do.'

Harris returned to sit next to Gallagher and leaned over to the sergeant.

'Maybe,' he said quietly, 'we've been looking at the wrong guy all the way along.'

'Maybe keep that quiet, eh?' said Gallagher. 'If he hears that, Robbie Graham's head will explode.'

'Ok, ladies and gentlemen,' said Raine, turning back to the board. 'Let's get this thing done.'

* * *

An hour later, the two northern detectives and Danny Raine were sitting in the terraced street where the garage stood. The officers were in an unmarked car hidden in the shadows at the far end of the street. Driving past the workshop earlier in the evening, Raine at the wheel, the officers had noticed that the front office window had been blacked out so that no one could see into the building but had noticed a faint glow from the interior. Now, as they waited, they felt a quickening of the pulse at the thought of the action to come.

'Are we sure they'll come?' asked Harris, who was in the passenger seat.

'Sure as we can be,' said Raine. 'Mind, we did wonder if de Luca's death would put the kybosh on things.'

'Who's your informant?' asked Gallagher.

'One of the girlfriends. She wants to leave him and reckons it will be easier if he's locked away.'

'So none of this came from de Luca?' asked Harris.

'No. I really have no idea where that one came from. I mean, you knew him, Hawk, can you really see him grassing anyone up to us?'

Harris shook his head. 'Not really,' he said.

'Anyway,' said Raine, 'it looks like our girl is right. GMP have identified three cars which were nicked in their area last night. Traffic spotted them on the M6 heading south, late this afternoon. They were a couple of miles apart but we are pretty sure they are travelling together.'

Their conversation was interrupted by the flash of headlights at the far end of the street and three cars drove slowly towards the garage. The green door swung open and the scene was briefly illuminated by lights from within. The detectives saw two men silhouetted as they stood on the pavement and gestured for the drivers to bring the vehicles in.

'Bingo,' breathed Raine. 'They're the ones that GMP reported stolen. A Mazda RX8, an Audi TT – that's the red one at the end, very nice motor, very nice motor indeed, nought to sixty in 5.3 seconds – and the other one is an Alfa Romeo Brera. That's class, that is. It's got a high double wishbone set-up with a multilink rear configuration. Very clever.'

'Yeah, and they increased the size of the coaxial damper spring,' said Gallagher. 'Smart move, I reckon. Definitely improved the handling, from what I hear.'

'I'm sorry,' said Harris, 'have we switched to a foreign language?'

'I take it you're not a petrolhead then?' said Raine.

'Sorry to disappoint you,' said the DCI as the first of the cars edged its way into the garage. 'What will happen to them now?'

'They'll get broken up.'

'Why? Surely, they are worth a lot of money in one piece.'

'You'd think, wouldn't you? But usually if gangs at this level try to sell a car on the black market, they might only get a few hundred for it.'

'What?' exclaimed the inspector as the final car eased itself gently through the door. 'But they must be worth thousands.'

'I know, sounds crazy, doesn't it?' said Raine. 'However, there is method in the madness because they are worth much more when they've been taken apart. See, you can get a grand for a car's automatic systems software alone, maybe more, and you can get another grand for the airbags and so on.'

'Yeah,' said Gallagher, 'it's cheaper than being ripped off by the manufacturers.'

'We reckon this lot sell the stuff on websites like eBay,' said Raine. 'Trouble is, it's virtually impossible to track something like that back – you really do need to nick them in the act.'

'Seems a pity to break up something like that,' said Harris as the last of the cars disappeared and the workshop door closed.

'It certainly is,' said Raine. 'You know we even heard reports of a couple of Ferraris making their way over here. We think Roscoe's gang has got a connection with someone in Italy. We assumed that was down to Paul de Luca, word is that one of the workers nicked them from the factory. It's in a place called Maranello.'

'I've been there,' said Gallagher. 'The Italian police arranged for us to do a behind-the-scenes tour.'

'Lucky basket,' replied Raine.

'So, when do we go in?' asked Harris, returning his attention to the garage.

'We'll give them time to start stripping them down.'

The chief inspector's mobile phone went off and he fished it out of his coat pocket.

'Harris,' he said.

'Guv,' said Alison Butterfield's voice. 'I've just been with Ralph. He's out of hospital now and says he has remembered more about what happened to him. Says he is convinced it was Garry Roscoe who attacked him. I told him what Davy Garbutt said and he confirmed that they were together when they saw him. What's more, he reckons Billy Dent will back up their story.'

'How come?'

'You know Billy said he saw a stranger on the hills the day de Luca was murdered? Well, according to Ralph, Billy recognised Garry Roscoe but was too frightened to tell anyone; they've had run-ins in the past, Garry used to do a bit of poaching when he was a lad, apparently.'

'Yeah, he did,' said Harris, deciding not to mention that he had accompanied him on more than one such occasions.

'What do you want me to do?' asked Butterfield.

'Go and see Billy.'

'What's that about?' asked Raine, as the DCI pocketed his phone again.

'That was one of my DCs,' said Harris, glancing back at Gallagher. 'She's now got three witnesses who can put Garry Roscoe in our neck of the woods. Is there a chance your surveillance guys could have lost him at some point?'

'I suppose it's always possible,' said Raine but he did not sound convinced. 'Look, I know Roscoe is a nasty piece of work but is he really capable of murdering someone?'

'Oh, aye. In fact, his brother vanished a few years ago and we are wondering if Garry did for him.' He glanced back at Gallagher. 'It was Matty who thought something was amiss. And nothing would surprise me with Garry Roscoe.'

'I take it you two have history?'

'I've waited years to get him for something,' nodded Harris, 'and I'm going to enjoy this.'

'Glad to oblige,' said Raine.

Raine's radio crackled.

'Go ahead,' said the DI

'It's Brian. Just heard back from Robbery – they're happy for us to lift Hopson as long as they get a crack at him as well.'

'Excellent,' said Raine. 'Go do it.'

'Right-oh, guv.'

'It's coming together,' said Raine cheerfully.

* * *

An hour later, he glanced at the clock on the dashboard and reached for his radio.

'Playtime, boys and girls,' he said.

The detectives got out of their car and walked slowly towards the workshop. As they neared, they could see, faintly through the darkened office window, that there were lights in the back of the building: peering closer they could just make out what looked like sparks. Raine placed his ear close to the garage door. The detectives could faintly hear hammering and the whine of an electric saw.

'They've definitely started,' he said.

Several cars drove slowly along the street behind them and pulled up outside the garage. A number of officers got out and walked over to join them. Others emerged from the shadows and soon there were more than a dozen men and women standing outside the garage, watching Raine expectantly.

'Everyone in position round the back?' he asked and one of the officers nodded.

Raine glanced at a couple of uniformed constables, who stepped forward with the hydraulic ram and placed it against the side door to the left of the main garage entrance. They hesitated for a moment or two as they readied themselves, then the door sprang open and the officers poured into the building. The air was filled with shouts and bangs as the team burst into the workshop to see several men in blue workmen's overalls clustered round one of the cars, which had already been stripped down. With alarmed cries, the men whirled round to face the police team. Two of them grabbed tyre irons and stepped forward.

'Drop them!' shouted Raine. 'This is a police raid and we don't want anyone to get hurt!'

The men hesitated than nodded and threw down the irons with a clanging sound which reverberated round the dimly-lit workshop. There was a sudden glint of metal and Gallagher realised that one of the other men had produced a knife. With a shout, the sergeant lunged forward and snapped out a hand, sending the knife flying and the man staggering backwards. Moments later, he was down on the floor, squealing in pain as his arms were cuffed behind his back by the sergeant. The incident unnerved the others and they meekly gave themselves up.

'Hang on,' said Harris, glancing around quickly, 'where's Roscoe?'

He whirled round to see, hiding in the shadows, the wiry figure of Garry Roscoe, whose eyes widened when they settled on Jack Harris.

'Hello, Garry,' said the chief inspector, taking a step forward. 'Long time, no see.'

'What the hell are you doing here?' exclaimed Roscoe.

'Wanted a little chat about the death of Paul de Luca,' replied Harris, extending a hand as he noticed that Roscoe had produced a screwdriver from his pocket. 'Put it down, Garry.'

Roscoe dived to one side and Harris noticed, for the first time, a side door which the fleeing man wrenched open to reveal a narrow flight of stairs going up into the darkness. The inspector hurled himself through the door in pursuit of his quarry. It was black on the staircase and Harris stopped for a few moments as his eyes grew accustomed to the darkness. A glancing blow sent him stumbling down the stairs. Shaking his head to clear his reeling senses, he could vaguely make out above him the figure of Garry Roscoe, who had reached the top and was pulling open another door through which streamed the dull orange glow of street lights. Harris staggered up the stairs and found himself on a flat roof at the rear of the garage. Roscoe had run to the edge and was peering down in alarm at the back alley full of police officers.

'Stay back!' Roscoe snarled, whirling round and jabbing the screwdriver at the approaching inspector. 'Stay back or I'll do you, Jack! I swear I will!'

'I don't think so, Garry,' said the inspector, regaining some of his composure as the shock of the punch wore off.

Roscoe seemed uncertain as to how to react, then lunged forward. Harris saw the screwdriver flash. The inspector swayed out of the way and flicked out an arm, the fist catching Roscoe with a shuddering uppercut that sent him sinking to his knees, where he crouched coughing up blood. Harris watched him impassively as he struggled to his feet, swaying slightly. Behind the inspector, there was the thundering sound of feet on the stairs and Gallagher and Raine burst out onto the roof but stopped as Harris held up a hand.

'He's mine,' he said and glanced round at the concerned look on the sergeant's face. 'Don't worry, Matty-lad. I know what I'm doing.'

'That's what worries me,' said the sergeant and made to move forward but Raine placed a restraining hand on his arm.

'I'm warning you,' cried Roscoe, spitting up blood. 'You know what I'm like, Jack.'

'I'm not some old dear, Garry. Come on, give it up. There's nowhere to run.'

With an enraged bellow, Roscoe hurled himself forward again. He did not even see the inspector's fist as it delivered a cold and clinical punch that harnessed all the inspector's controlled aggression to drive deep into the solar plexus. Roscoe's face registered shock before his knees buckled and he sprawled on the floor, battling desperately for breath.

'That's for Emily Carlisle,' said Harris, standing over him. 'Should have done it at the time.'

It was several moments before Roscoe was able to look up at the detective and when he did, the hatred flashed in his eyes and he started to haul himself unsteadily to his feet. Harris held up another hand as Raine and Gallagher moved forward.

'They don't get up from that,' he said.

For a moment, it looked as it Roscoe was going to try another assault but then the waves of pain overwhelmed him and he grunted, sank back to his knees and the screwdriver clattered to the floor. Then he lay still.

'You know,' said Harris, walking past the officers. 'I've been wanting to do that for more than thirty years.'

Chapter twelve

Jack Harris was in a good mood as he strode down the corridor towards the interview room an hour later. The arrested men had been brought back to the local police station and, after a hurried discussion between the chief inspector and Danny Raine, the DI had agreed to let Harris sit in on the interrogation of Roscoe. Now, as he prepared to push open the door, Harris hesitated and allowed himself a smile. He was going to enjoy this. Ever since he had watched in horror as Emily Carlisle had fallen to the floor in Levton Bridge market place all those years ago, he had known deep down that this day would eventually come, and that when it did he would be on one side and Garry Roscoe on the other.

The inspector had always looked on the pensioner's passing as the defining moment in his life, the incident that steered him back along the right path when it would have been only to easy to slide into crime. He knew his father had felt that way, a belief that had made him seek to get his son away from the influence of Paul de Luca and Garry Roscoe, a belief that if the teenage Harris had stayed in Levton Bridge it would not be long before he stood alongside them in a courtroom dock. In time, Harris had come to realise the same truth: his time away in the Army gave him time to think and he had recalled many times the pain on his father's face when the police came to their house to take his son away for questioning about the attack on the pensioner. Harris also remembered the angry confrontation the night after Emily Carlisle died when her son hammered on the front door, the tears streaming down his face and demanding to see the teenager so that he could vent his anger. He relived how his father had remonstrated with the visitor – there had been raised voices for several minutes – while the young Harris had cowered in his bedroom, tears coursing down his cheeks. In that moment, as he heard the door slam and peered tentatively out of the window at the retreating back of the furious son, the young Jack Harris had resolved never to place his father in such a situation again. Never to be a coward. And never to allow anyone else to make the decisions, as he had done with Garry Roscoe.

Perhaps, the inspector thought now, as his hand still rested on the door handle, it had been the defining moment in Garry Roscoe's life as well. Harris recalled the way Roscoe had gloated about escaping prosecution for manslaughter after he was released from his sentence for the handbag snatch. It was in that moment, thought the inspector, recalling Robert de Luca's words, that Roscoe selected the path he was to walk. The DCI pushed open the door and stood in amazement as he surveyed Ella Reynolds sitting next to a glowering Garry Roscoe. She smiled at his reaction.

'Hello, Jack,' she said.

Raine, who was sitting at the table, looked at Harris and raised an eyebrow.

'You two know each other?' he asked.

'She represented Gerald Hopson when we lifted him last week,' said Harris and gave the lawyer a strange look.

'I understand you have arrested him again,' said Reynolds. 'I'll give you one thing, Chief Inspector, you never give up.'

'No, I don't. Would you care to explain how you are acting for Garry as well?'

'I get to meet all the nicest people.'

Roscoe smirked. Harris did not reply but sat down at the table.

'Right,' said Raine briskly. 'We have a lot to talk about and time is getting on so might I suggest that we make a start.'

'You can start by telling me why Jack Harris is here,' said Reynolds calmly. 'To the best of my knowledge, this is not his case.'

'We think Garry may be implicated in the death of Paul de Luca,' said Harris, 'and possibly those of William Hadleigh and Eddy Rawmarsh as well.'

'I heard about it on the television,' she nodded. 'Such an unfortunate incident but one that has nothing to do with Mr Roscoe.'

'According to our people, the brakes were doctored by someone with an in-depth knowledge of the way cars work. Do you know anyone like that, Garry?' The inspector fixed Roscoe with a stare.

'You're fishing,' said Roscoe. 'I ain't got anything to do with any of this. I have no idea who those blokes are and I ain't even been in Levton Bridge for two years.'

'We've got witnesses say you're lying, including the man you assaulted.'

'Assaulted who?' asked Reynolds, unsettled by the inspector's persistent line of questioning and glancing at an alarmed client.

'A man called Ralph Corbett,' said Harris.

'Him!' snorted Roscoe, 'I ain't seen that old gobshite for years. I'm telling the truth, honest I am, Hawk.'

'That's DCI Harris to you,' said the detective. 'Then we might want to ask you a few questions about what happened to your brother.'

Garry looked at him uneasily.

'Come on Garry,' said Harris. 'It really is time to start telling the truth because I am not in the mood for games and neither, I imagine, is Detective Inspector Raine.'

Raine shook his head.

'I think we need a quick break,' said Reynolds.

Leaving lawyer and client to discuss their next move, the two detectives went back to Danny Raine's office, where the detective inspector brewed up some tea and the men slumped wearily into chairs and sat in silence for a few moments as they sipped their drinks.

'Sorry,' said Harris eventually.

'For what?'

'For messing up your interview with all that stuff – this is your show, after all, and I had no right to...'

'It seemed to unsettle him so it may work in our favour. Frankly, we have got him bang to rights – we've got surveillance stuff coming out of our backsides.'

There was silence for a few moments as the men continued to drink their tea then Raine looked at Harris.

'Look, don't take this the wrong way,' he said slowly, 'but are you sure you are right about Roscoe being in your patch?'

'Our witnesses seem certain.'

'Trouble is, I'd say the same for my lot,' said Raine, reaching into a drawer to produce a sheaf of papers, 'and they are adamant that he has not left London during all the time we have been watching him. Take this, for example – these are our surveillance records for the past six days.'

He stared flicking through the documents.

'We had positive IDs on a number of occasions,' said Raine. 'That was a report from the night your bloke Corbett was attacked.'

Raine handed over a document.

'As you can see,' he said, 'our lot have Garry drinking at The Mitre until late. There is no way he was in Levton Bridge.'

Harris pursed his lips but before he could reply, there was a knock on the open door and in walked one of Raine's detectives.

'Tracked down these photos you wanted, guv,' he said, handing over a brown packet before disappearing back into the corridor.

'Thanks,' said Raine, pulling out the pictures and holding them up so that Harris could see. 'That's him leaving the pub. Pissed as a rat, apparently. The other two guys are a couple of those we lifted tonight. Randall and Logan. The lads with the tyre irons.'

Harris stared at the picture for a few moments.

'I've got more where that came from,' added Raine. 'Sorry, Hawk, but I'm not buying your lads' story, ex coppers or not.'

Harris placed the surveillance reports on the desk and fished his phone out of his suit pocket.

'Alison,' he said a few moments later, 'have you been able to get hold of Billy Dent?'

'Sorry, guv. It's really bad weather up here, there's snow on the tops and according to old man Jessop, Billy sometimes stays up there to keep an eye on the sheep when it's bad. Some little cottage or something.'

'Metcalfe's,' said Harris. 'If it's snowing, you'll not get him tonight.'

'I asked if the place had a phone but it doesn't. I'll try to get up there in the morning.'

'No, leave it,' said Harris. 'I'll talk to Billy when I get back. He's a curmudgeonly old git at the best of times but if he's going to talk to anyone, it will be me. Anything else I need to know?'

'I'll put the DI on.'

'Hello, guv,' she said.

'Working late.'

'You know how it is.'

'Sorry,' said Harris.

'That's fifty-nine times you've apologised,' said Roberts. 'Just remember you owe me six days somewhere nice and sunny. How's it going down there?'

'Slow. And you?'

'Lots of flak flying. Curtis is on the verge of having a stroke, Barry Ramsden's phone bill must be horrendous and the vicar mentioned you in his sermon. Apparently, you are the Devil incarnate, something I had always suspected, of course, but could never prove.'

'Marvellous,' chuckled Harris.

There was silence for a few moments.

'Look,' said Roberts, 'I know Ralph Corbett is a good friend but are you sure about him.' There was hesitation in her voice. 'I mean, really sure?'

Harris glanced down at the surveillance pictures strewn across the desk but before he could answer the question there was another knock on the door and a uniformed constable walked in.

'Roscoe's lawyer wants to talk to you,' he said.

Harris was relieved to end the phone call but he knew that he would have to answer the question some time. Back in the interview room, he tried to focus on the matter in hand as he stared across the desk at Ella Reynolds and Garry Roscoe.

'My client is prepared to admit to being involved in the car thefts,' said Reynolds. 'He sees little sense in trying to deny his involvement.'

'I would say he is right,' said Raine.

'I am sure you would,' said Reynolds and glanced at Harris. 'However, my client wishes it to be known that he strenuously denies knowing anything about these other matters.'

Roscoe nodded vigorously.

'But isn't it true that you thought Paul de Luca was a grass?' said Harris, uncomfortably aware that he was

156

starting to sound desperate. 'I mean, that must have really hacked you off, Garry. I know it would if I were in your shoes. After all, it would have wrecked your little car scam.'

'I heard the rumours,' said Roscoe. 'We all did but I didn't believe them. Do you really think Paul de Luca would grass anyone up to the police? He hated you all.'

'Yes, but…'

'Look, I had nothing to do with de Luca's death,' said Roscoe in measured tones, sensing the inspector's difficulty. 'If you think otherwise, you'll have to prove it.'

'And I can't help feeling that you are already pushing your luck, Chief Inspector,' said Ella Reynolds. 'And how this interview proceeds will have a major bearing on whether or not we proceed with an allegation of assault against you – we do feel that you used unnecessary force against my client up on the roof.'

'Not the first time you have tried that one, Ms Reynolds,' said Danny Raine.

Reynolds smiled at him sweetly. The door opened and Matty Gallagher walked in.

'Can I have a word, guv?' he asked solemnly.

Harris fired a dark look at Garry Roscoe then went out into the corridor.

'Well?' he asked grumpily.

'Sorry,' said Gallagher, 'but I have been through their surveillance logs since the operation began, and there's no way he left London.'

'Not at all?' asked Harris in a hollow voice.

'Not all. There's another alternative. But it requires an open mind on the subject.'

'Go on, say it,' said Harris, looking at him sharply. 'Open mind about what?'

'On whether or not Ralph Corbett is lying.'

Harris walked a few paces along the corridor then turned and rested his head on the wall before turning dark eyes on the sergeant.

'Lying about what?' asked Harris.

'Everything.'

Harris said nothing but walked back into the interview room to stare balefully at Garry Roscoe.

'We need to check out your story,' said the DCI.

'In which case, might I suggest,' said Raine, keen to press home his advantage while Roscoe's mind was focused on other things, 'that we take Garry's statement about the auto-crime now and reconvene first thing in the morning on the other issues.'

'That is fine by me,' said Reynolds, 'but I would like a few minutes with Gerald Hopson first.'

'So would I,' said Harris darkly.

Ten minutes later, she was sitting in another interview room, next to Gerald Hopson.

'You keep cropping up like a bad penny, Gerald,' said the inspector.

'I have done nothing wrong and you have no right holding me,' said Hopson with unaccustomed spirit. 'This is harassment.'

'Another of our Ms Reynold's favourite words,' said Raine dryly.

Reynolds gave another sweet smile.

'I'm sure it is,' said Harris and looked hard at Hopson. 'I take it you know that Eddy Rawmarsh is dead, Gerald?'

'What of it?'

'Well, with Paul de Luca gone as well, that just leaves you from that day in the quarry. To carry the can, as it were.'

Hopson looked worried but said nothing and continued to say nothing for a further hour until a weary detective chief inspector returned to the auto-crime squad room to sit gazing bleakly out over the twinkling lights of London. The inspector's thoughts turned to Garry Roscoe. Despite himself, he had to admit that it seemed unlikely that Roscoe was the murderer of Paul de Luca or had anything to do with doctoring the Jaguar's brakes. With him out of the frame, the inspector's mind focused in on Hopson and his criminal connections. Convinced that he was somehow involved, the inspector nevertheless found himself frustrated at his inability to exact a confession from him. And then there was the story told by Ralph Corbett and Davy Garbutt. Why on earth would they lie? Harris frowned: he knew the answer to that one and it was time to deal with it. It was time to bring it to an end.

Hearing the click of heels on the polished corridor floor outside the squad room, the inspector twisted in his seat to see Ella Reynolds standing at the door.

'Oh, it's you,' he said.

'Don't be like that, Jack' said Ella Reynolds. 'It's only a game.'

Harris said nothing and she walked over to him, so close that he could smell her perfume.

'I know this place,' she said in a low voice, 'where they have sixty-eight different brands of whisky. You'd like it, Jack, you really would.'

'Are you propositioning me?' asked the inspector looking up at her. 'Again?'

'Like I said,' replied Reynolds. 'It's only a game.'

* * *

Shortly after seven-thirty the next evening, the northbound train started to climb into the Pennines. As the inspector looked out over the dim shapes of the looming foothills in the fading light, he smiled and started to relax for the first time in twenty-four hours. Despite the adrenaline rush of the raid, it was good to be going home. There were too many temptations in London. Too many mistakes to be made. As he stared out of the window, it seemed to the inspector that he could still smell Ella Reynold's perfume lingering in the air. He closed his eyes and tried to think of other things.

And there was plenty to think about. Harris and his sergeant had spent the first part of the morning questioning a stubborn Garry Roscoe, Harris declining to meet the gaze of Ella Reynolds over the table. The tension between the two was not lost on Gallagher, but the sergeant said nothing. The interview with Garry Roscoe terminated, Harris and Raine had gone in to see Gerald Hopson. However, guided by Ella Reynolds, the nervy Hopson had parried every question and with nothing to link him to the stolen car racket and no fresh evidence in relation to the deaths in the north, the detectives had sent him back to the cells.

That was when Harris took the decision to return to Levton Bridge and leave Gallagher to handle inquiries in the capital. The catalyst for the decision was a phone call from Gillian Roberts, who said that Curtis was becoming increasingly agitated about the lack of progress in the investigation and had hinted darkly at serious matters to discuss with the inspector. Despite his unwillingness to discuss anything with the superintendent, Harris nevertheless needed no second bidding to pack his bags and within an hour was on the train, grateful that he did not see Ella Reynolds as he left the police station.

Throughout the journey, he kept coming back to one thought, one that had struck him the moment he had first walked into the interview room to question Garry Roscoe and seen Ella Reynolds sitting there. Same lawyer. Harris sensed that it meant something, something more than the simple process of legal representation, but he was not sure what. And each time he thought about it, he thought about Gerald Hopson. Where did he fit in with things? Surely, the meek financial advisor was not capable of murder. As the train rolled north, the inspector turned the thought over and over in his mind but failed to come up with a resolution. Nevertheless, he had the strong sense that he was close to a breakthrough, that he was missing just one piece of information to put the jigsaw together.

Now, exhausted by his thinking, he sat, dozing lightly in his seat, the effects of his disrupted night catching up with him and making him feel increasingly weary. An hour and half later, he jerked awake, glanced out of the window to see through the gathering darkness the approaching lights of Levton Bridge. The inspector peered closer and noted that the snow had largely melted and was now only a light dusting on the fields. With a smile on his face, he reached up to bring down his overnight bag. Walking along the carriage, he peered out and saw Butterfield standing on the platform, Scoot sitting at her feet. Harris beamed.

'Am I glad to see you!' he exclaimed as he bounded along the platform and threw his arms round the excited dog.

'And there was me thinking you were talking about me,' said Butterfield with a slight smile.

'Always happy to see you, my dear,' said the inspector, not looking up from Scoot.

'How was Ella?' asked the constable as the officers started to walk along the platform.

'There,' said Harris, 'you had to go and ruin it. Come on, Constable, let's see if we can't find Billy Dent.'

'Welcome back, Jacky boy,' said the man, shrinking back into the shadows as they walked past him on the platform.

As Harris was sitting in the CID room half an hour later, catching up with Gillian Roberts and Butterfield, a Range Rover containing two men edged its way slowly up the track leading to Howgill Farm ten miles to the north-west. The vehicle had made its way along the deserted road skirting Dead Hill before turning through a gateway and, with headlights dipped, edging its way up the winding little path; the driver concentrating hard as he negotiated every little twist and turn, the only sound, small stones ricocheting onto the vehicle's underside. After a few minutes, the driver brought the Range Rover to a halt close to some trees and cut the lights altogether. Through the darkness, the men could see the farmhouse a hundred metres further up the slope, snuggled in the lee of the hill. The lights were on and the men could see shadowy figures moving about through the thin living room curtains.

'Two,' said the man in the passenger seat.

'Three,' replied the driver.

The passenger looked again.

'Three,' he agreed. 'Sorry.'

Without acknowledging the comment, the driver reached into the back seat and produced two sawn-off shotguns, handing one of them to the passenger, then reaching over to the glove compartment and bringing out two balaclava masks. The men pulled them over their heads in silence then glanced across at each other. Wordlessly, they checked their weapons before clambering out of the vehicle.

The men's feet made little sound as they walked across the grass with its thin layer of snow. At one point, a sheep in the adjoining fields bleated loudly and the men halted, standing motionless, acutely conscious of their beating hearts. Seeing no sign of anyone peering through the window of the house, they relaxed then continued their stealthy approach.

In the living room, old man Jessop was pouring out two glasses of whisky, one of which he handed to his shepherd. Billy Dent's flat cap sat on the dining table, the crumb-flecked white tablecloth testament to the meal they had just eaten. As the men raised the glasses to their lips, clinking sounds from the kitchen told them that Jessop's wife, Edna, had started the washing up.

'Should I help?' began Dent, glancing towards the door.

'Nay, she'll be alright,' replied Jessop, downing his whisky. 'Drink up, Billy lad, ye've got time for another?'

Dent downed his drink and proffered up his glass. Jessop picked up the bottle from the table. As he did, a sound paused his hand.

'Did you hear that?' he asked.

Billy Dent listened.

'I heard nowt,' he said.

'There it is again,' said Jessop, hearing as sharp as ever despite his seventy-nine years. 'There's someone out there.'

Before either of them could react, there was crashing sound as the front door was kicked in, followed by shouting as the masked men burst into the room, brandishing shotguns.

'Don't move!' rasped the driver.

Jessop and Dent gaped at them, too shocked to react. Jessop's wife rushed out of the kitchen but cowered back at the sight of the guns. Dent's collie dog scrambled up from its resting place by the fire and started to growl. The driver glared at it.

'Make it shut up!' he snarled, waggling the shotgun at Dent.

'Quiet, lad,' said Dent, trying to control the tremor in his voice, and the dog stopped growling, backed away and lay low to the carpet, never taking his eye off the gunmen.

The driver turned back to Jessop, and noticed the farmer's eyes sliding towards the corner of the room where his own shotgun was propped up against the wall.

'Don't even think about it,' rasped the driver.

'What do you want?' asked the farmer, a hint of defiance in his voice as he felt a rising anger that these men should threaten him into his own home. 'We've got nothing of value here.'

'Don't try it on!' snapped the driver. 'We know about the jewellery.'

'What jewellery?' asked Jessop.

'I only have a brooch my mother gave me,' said Edna, who was still standing in the kitchen doorway. 'And that's not worth much. Are you sure you have got the right house?'

The robbers glanced at each other, seeming to hesitate for a moment.

'Show him,' said the driver, gesturing to Edna with his gun then pointing to his accomplice.

For the next few minutes, Jessop and Bill Dent stood in the living room and listened to the sound of the accomplice ransacking the bedrooms, wrenching drawers out and letting them fall to the floor, ripping wardrobe doors open and pulling the linen of the beds as he searched beneath the mattresses. Occasionally, they heard his raised voice but the shotgun pointed at them by the accomplice meant neither man moved. Eventually, the accomplice came down, Edna walking before him, her face drained of blood as he jabbed the gun into her back. The accomplice pushed her roughly into the room.

'Hang on a minute,' began Jessop as his wife cried out and stumbled into the armchair, but a flick of the gun from the driver silenced him.

'This is no time for heroes,' said the driver then glanced at his accomplice. 'Well?'

'Nothing,' said the accomplice.

The driver turned to Jessop. 'So where is it, old man?'

Jessop shook his head. 'There ain't no jewellery,' he said. 'Edna's telling the truth.'

The driver nodded at his accomplice who started searching the room, ripping out drawers and flinging seat cushions across the floor. Once he had finished, he went into the kitchen and repeated the process: the others could hear the slamming of wooden doors and the smashing crockery. Edna started to sob.

'Shut it!' snarled the driver, holding the shotgun to her head.

'Now come on, lads,' said Billy Dent, taking a step forward.

The driver spun round and pointed the gun at Dent. There was a deafening noise and the shepherd gave a gasp and slumped to his knees, blood spurting from a wound in his chest.

'What you doing?' cried the accomplice in horror, running back in from the kitchen.

He stared down at the prostrate man then looked up at his driver, who seemed rooted to the spot, gaping at the dying shepherd. Jessop took a step forward and the accomplice lashed out with his gun, catching the old man full in the face with the butt and sending him flying over the table and into the dresser, which rocked and swayed for a few moments, cascading plates and dishes down onto the unconscious farmer. Edna cried out in horror and rushed over to him.

'Come on,' said the accomplice, taking a quick look at the prone form of Billy Dent, then grasping the driver by the arm.

'It was an accident,' said the driver, gaping down at Billy Dent. 'He startled me, it just went off.'

'Come on!' shouted his accomplice, starting to drag him towards the door then looking back at the weeping Edna, crouched over her motionless husband. 'Let's get out of here before she calls the police.'

Then they were gone into the night.

* * *

Harris and Butterfield were already on their way to Jessop's farm in search of Billy Dent when the call came in. Harris sped his Land Rover round bends, Butterfield's knuckles glowing white as she held onto the dashboard and Scoot protesting as he was thrown around in the back. No words were said on the journey as the officers listened to the constant radio traffic spreading word of the shooting. The detectives arrived at the farm within twenty-five minutes, bumping and rocking up the track at speed to be confronted by a patrol car parked outside the house, its blue flashing light illuminating the darkness, and an ambulance crew carrying Jessop out of his home on a stretcher, a weeping Edna walking beside him, holding her husband's hand.

Harris slewed his vehicle to halt beside the house and leapt out, flashing his ID card at the ambulance officers and glancing down at Jessop, whose eyes were closed and whose pale features were rivered with trickles of blood from a gash on his forehead. Harris motioned for Butterfield to take Edna away and when the constable had guided the distraught woman back into the house, glanced at the ambulance crew.

'Will he live?' he asked.

'Depends how strong he is,' replied the female paramedic carrying the back of the stretcher.

'Strong as they come,' said Harris, looking back down at the unconscious farmer.

'Then he's got a chance,' said the woman, nodding back at the house. 'But we couldn't do anything for the other one. Sorry.'

She helped her colleague load Jessop into the back of their vehicle. Butterfield, noticing them prepare for departure, guided Edna back out of the house and helped her into the rear of the ambulance, where she sat by her husband, once more holding his hand and unable to hold back the tears. That done, the constable walked back into the house where Jack Harris was standing in the living room and staring down grimly at the crumpled body of Billy Dent with the blood welling from the gaping hole in his chest.

Harris felt the strange detached feeling that always came when he was confronted with death: he had seen enough bodies not to be shocked. It was the same feeling he had experienced when he killed his first man as a soldier. It was difficult to describe – not that he had ever confided in many people – but the best description he could come up with was a sense that Jack Harris was elsewhere and that someone else was occupying his body. It was such a feeling that now allowed him to cope with Billy Dent's death. The same could not be said of the two uniformed officers who stood silently in the corner of the room: the younger of the two looked very pale indeed. Butterfield nodded to them but none of them spoke. Each one needed time to compose their thoughts. Harris glanced at the detective constable as she came to stand next to him.

'This your first murder?' he asked.

Butterfield nodded.

'Then this will be good experience for you,' said Harris, noticing her expression. 'For a start, we need forensics up here, and a pathologist. Oh, and get Robbie Graham. Gillian will need all the help she can get when she arrives.'

Butterfield nodded, reached for her radio and walked out into the narrow little hallway. Harris could hear her talking in a low voice.

'You two,' he said, turning to the uniformed officers. 'I want the path taped off down on the main road. The last thing we want is the world and his dog tramping in here.'

He noticed the officers glance at Scoot, who had just wandered into the room from the kitchen where he had been sniffing around for scraps.

'Except that one,' said Harris with a slight smile. 'Go on, get the tape sorted. No one gets up here without my say so. Is that clear? Oh, and I want roadblocks on every road out of this valley. Everyone gets stopped. No one slips through.'

The officers took a final glance at the body of Billy Dent and headed for the front door. Alone in the room with the corpse, Jack Harris stared down at him thoughtfully.

'Somehow I don't think I can pin this one on Gerald Hopson,' he murmured.

The inspector walked over to the window and stared out into the night, watching the lights of the ambulance bouncing down the rough little track then reaching the road, quickening their pace and disappearing from view. In the distance, Harris could see the approaching lights of police cars. Glancing closer to the cottage, he saw the two uniformed officers jogging down the track towards the road. The inspector looked back into the room and cursed beneath his breath: life was getting too complicated for his liking. No days off bird-watching, no tramping the moors with Scoot for a while, not while this was going off. However, there was another, stronger thought on his mind and it was a much more troubling one. Yet again, the peace, the sanctity, of Dead Hill had been shattered by the actions of others, and the inspector hated the idea. The hill had always occupied a special place in his life, it was what brought him back to the area as he sought the peace that eluded him for too long. It was where he had chosen to make his home but now, something had changed and the realisation that the cause could be one of his oldest friends hit him hard.

Standing in the cottage, Jack Harris was confronted with the reality of the situation. Feeling the rage building within him, and recognising the danger signs, the detective chief inspector took deep breaths: it was one of the techniques he had been taught in the Army. Guilty of assaulting a sergeant one drunken night in Germany early in his military career, the young Harris had been sent to anger management classes. Because there had been several such incidents, he was warned that the classes represented his last chance. Standing now in the cottage, he could hear the instructor's calming words as he persuaded the young squaddie to confront his inner demons, the anger at what had happened to Emily Carlisle, the self-loathing at the way he had stood by and let it happen, the guilt at the pain his actions had caused his parents. Harris heard once again the instructor's advice that he should always try, at times of extreme provocation, to conjure up images of their times together. The inspector doubted that he could ever have had such a scenario in mind. Recalling the advice to transport his mind to a place of pleasant memories, Harris imagined himself walking the hills with Scoot and slowly found himself calming down and his head beginning to clear. He turned away from the window as Butterfield walked into the room, slipping the radio into her coat pocket.

'All done,' she said, then noticing the inspector's slightly flushed expression, asked, 'You ok, guv?'

'Yeah. Just been walking the dog.'

'Guv?' said the constable, glancing over at Scoot, who was sitting in the corner of the room and watching his master intently.

'Nothing,' said Harris and gestured to Billy Dent. 'Any thoughts, Constable?'

Butterfield hesitated.

'Come on,' said Harris, 'We're both thinking it.'

'Ok,' said Butterfield, also looking at the body and feeling a sense of relief as her nausea abated and her detective's instincts returned. 'I am thinking that Billy Dent was the only other person to have claimed to have seen Garry Roscoe up here. With him dead, we only have the words of Ralph Corbett and Davy Garbutt for it – what if they are in it together? I mean, they are old friends.'

'I think,' said Harris, turning to look out over the darkened hills again and noticing the car lights making their way up the track. 'That looks like the DI. Maybe it is time for us to go see what our Mister Corbett has to say.'

Chapter thirteen

Harris and Butterfield made the journey to Levton Bridge in silence, both alone with their thoughts as the inspector guided the Land Rover along darkened country roads. Sitting alongside him, Butterfield stared out of the window, occasionally glancing over at the inspector, but saying nothing: it did not seem the time and there did not seem to be the words. As the detectives approached Levton Bridge, they saw a dull orange glow in the sky.

'That's Corbett's place!' exclaimed Harris.

He jabbed his foot onto the accelerator and within minutes, they were screeching to a halt outside the animal sanctuary. Jumping out of the vehicle, the detectives could hear the crackle of flames and the squeal of terrified pigs and, drifting through the night air, the sound of approaching sirens. Ignoring the thick smoke, the officers ran into the centre but Butterfield sunk to her knees, gagging at the sickening stench of burning flesh. Kneeling there, trying to catch her breath and spitting to banish the taste from her mouth, she watched as the inspector sprinted towards the blazing cabin.

'Jack!' came a frantic voice.

Harris whirled round to be confronted by a weeping Maureen running down one of the paths.

'He's in there!' she cried, pointing to the cabin, 'Ralph's in there!'

Harris took one look at the inferno, lunged forward and kicked the cabin door open. Flames leapt out into the night air and the inspector felt the intense heat searing the skin on his face. He staggered backwards then, covering his head with his coat, dived back in. Once inside, he could just make out through the dancing flames the motionless figure of a man slumped in the office chair. Harris cried out and moved forward but there was a tearing sound and part of the cabin's roof caved in, catching him a glancing blow and sending him crashing to his knees. For a few moments, the dazed inspector struggled to regain his senses, aware only of the heat. Shaking his head, he tried to clamber to his feet but staggered backwards before becoming vaguely aware of strong hands dragging him out into the night air.

'Leave this to us, Jack,' said a firefighter.

Harris nodded and lay on the floor, staring up through at the clear night sky glimpsed through the swirling smoke. After struggling to catch his breath for several moments, he got unsteadily to his feet and watched grimly as the fire crew trained their jets of water on the cabin. Within a short time, the flames died down and the smoke started to subside and the crew was able to get inside. Harris walked unsteadily over to where Butterfield was consoling a weeping Maureen Corbett.

'What the hell happened?' asked the inspector weakly.

'Two men,' said Maureen, battling back the tears. 'They came to the house looking for Ralph. They tried to take him. I tried to stop them but they both had shotguns.'

Harris noticed the ugly gash on her forehead.

'Did they do that?' he asked.

She nodded.

'I lost consciousness for a few seconds. When I came to, I…' Her voice tailed off and she looked away from the gutted cabin.

One of the firefighters walked across to the detectives.

'I'm truly sorry,' he said, looking at Maureen. 'There really was nothing we could do.'

Maureen gave an unearthly wail.

'Take her back to the house,' said Harris, glancing at Butterfield.

Having watched the constable lead Maureen away, the inspector returned his gaze to the firefighters as they started wading through the wreckage of the building. Harris heard his mobile phone ring and fished it out of his coat pocket.

'This had better be good,' he said.

'Not sure you'll like it,' said Gallagher's voice. 'But I've finished double-checking everything down here and I really do think we have to ask ourselves if Ralph Corbett was telling the truth about Roscoe being up there. Maybe we need to get him in for a little chat.'

'That may be a little difficult,' replied Harris, watching the firefighters sifting through the shell of the cabin.

'Why?'

'Tell you in a minute. You got anything else for me?'

'As a matter of fact, I have, guv. See, the surveillance lads have been monitoring Roscoe's phone calls. We guess most of them were made on untraceable mobiles but he did make some on his home phone.'

'And?'

'And he's kept in touch with an old friend.'

* * *

Less than an hour later, Harris was knocking on the front door of Edith Roscoe's cottage.

'Hawk,' she said with a welcoming smile, ushering him into the living room. 'You've been too much of a stranger.'

'I'm sorry to come so late.'

'You said on the phone it was important.'

'I have a question for you,' said the inspector, walking over to the little side table and gazing down at the school photograph.

After scanning the faces staring up at him, the chief inspector held up the picture and placed a finger on one of boys, spending a few moments staring into the features, at the smile he knew so well, the smile that had not changed down all the years he had known him. Harris shook his head in disbelief then held the picture up so that Edith could see the boy to whom he was pointing.

'Was he there the day Garry had the row with Jimmy?' he asked then jabbed a finger at another of the boys. 'With him?'

'No.'

'I think you're lying to protect him.'

She looked away and stared into the fire.

'If he was there,' she said, 'I am sure he would never have hurt him.'

Harris looked back down at the face staring out of the photograph.

'Maybe,' he said. 'Maybe.'

* * *

The next morning, with the corridors of the London police station still largely deserted, Matty Gallagher walked into the interview room and surveyed Gerald Hopson, who was sitting at the table and eying the sergeant nervously: his pale expression suggested that he had slept little in the cell. Ella Reynolds looked up as the detective entered and sat down.

'I take it you have a good reason for dragging me in at this unearthly hour?' she said irritably.

'Yeah, I'm sorry about that,' nodded Gallagher, 'but the custody officer wants me to clear a couple of cells and I imagine Mr Hopson here would like to get it all over with.'

'Get what over with?' asked Reynolds.

173

Hopson looked at him hopefully.

'Look, this is embarrassing for me,' said Gallagher. 'Your client is free to go.'

Hopson heaved a sigh of relief.

'Why the change of heart?' asked Reynolds, recovering from her surprise.

'There have been developments,' replied the sergeant uncomfortably.

'What developments?'

'I am afraid I cannot say,' replied the sergeant, gesturing to the door. 'Mr Hopson, I am truly sorry that we have put you through this distressing experience. DCI Harris has asked me to convey the force's apologies for the inconvenience. There would seem to have been an unfortunate misunderstanding.'

'Just like that?' said Hopson, anger quickly replacing relief. 'After all I have gone through?'

'Like I said,' replied the sergeant, 'we are very sorry.'

'I should think so,' said Hopson. 'Do you know what it's like cooped up in a police cell for day after day? In fact…'

'I think the sergeant is aware of your views,' said Reynolds, holding up a hand. 'Wait for me in the reception area, Gerald. We can decide how best to proceed on this matter later. I think the sergeant appreciates that there will be legal repercussions.'

Hopson looked as if he was about to remonstrate with her then nodded meekly and left the room, followed by a uniformed officer who ushered him along the corridor. When he had gone, Reynolds eyed the sergeant across the table.

'This is all very sudden, Sergeant. Are you going to tell me what has made you change your mind?'

'I'm not sure I really should.'

'Come on, Matty,' said the solicitor. 'You know you can trust me.'

Gallagher considered the comment for a few moments then nodded.

'Harris seems to,' he said, lowering his voice. 'Look, between you and me, we've got someone for the murders.'

'Who?'

'Not sure I can really say that.'

'Come on,' said Reynolds, leaning forward. 'I won't tell anyone.'

The sergeant was aware of the aroma of her perfume drifting across the table. It reminded him of an old girlfriend.

'Ok,' he said, 'but you did not get this from me, right?'

She nodded.

'Ralph Corbett.'

Reynolds gave a low whistle. 'But I thought he was an ex-copper,' she said.

'He is and what's more, he is a good friend of the DCI. That's what makes it so embarrassing.' The sergeant looked at her unhappily. 'What's more, we think he was working with another former copper. Chap called Davy Garbutt. There's going to be hell to pay. It's going to destroy the DCI's career. Any chance you can go easy on us?'

'I may have no option in the matter,' said Reynolds, her eyes gleaming. 'My first responsibility is to my clients. I take it this Corbett fellow has confessed?'

'It's not that easy, I am afraid. Ralph Corbett died in a fire last night. We are pretty sure he started it himself – the governor reckons he was trying to get rid of evidence, and that it went wrong. Garbutt is missing but we'll get him – he can't have gone far.'

'Interesting,' breathed Reynolds, who stood up, closed her briefcase and extended a gloved hand. 'Well, thank you for letting me know. Maybe we will meet another time.'

'Who knows?' said Gallagher as he watched her walk from the room and listened to her heels clicking along the deserted corridor. 'Who knows?'

As Ella Reynolds headed for the reception area, she passed Danny Raine heading the other way. Having reached the interview room, the detective inspector waited by the door and watched her disappear round a corner and listened as the sound of her heels faded away down the stairs. Once she had gone, he walked into the interview room.

'I hope your governor is right about this,' he said to Gallagher, his voice betraying his anxiety. 'If we cock this up, there will be people wanting to string him up by his short and curlies.'

'Yeah, go on,' said Gallagher bleakly, 'make me feel better.'

* * *

Levton Bridge police station was a hive of activity. Officers walked briskly around its corridors, imbued with a renewed sense of purpose, and there was an almost physical tension in the air: the events of the past week had sent a frisson of excitement around a building where the more usual preoccupation was Friday night pub brawls in the market place and shed break-ins.

If the killings had changed the atmosphere in the police station, they had also confirmed the dramatic change in Jack Harris. As in London, he noticed it again in himself now as he busied himself making sure that the inquiry was being run properly, briefing his detectives and devising fresh lines of investigation. Officers commented on the energy that he exuded and how he had instilled in them a sense of confidence that the crimes would soon be solved.

For all his re-awakened enthusiasm, Jack Harris preferred to work quietly and was not the public face of the investigation. That role had been assumed ever since the death of Paul de Luca by Superintendent Curtis, and the DCI was happy to let that continue. He watched with mild amusement as Curtis strode round the station, barking out instructions and demanding updates from officers. Curtis also insisted on handling the media, giving interviews to the reporters who had decamped to the town over recent days. Always irked when the journalists asked for Jack Harris, Curtis had continually dismissed their requests: no one was going to ruin this for him. Or at least that was how Harris read the situation. Everyone knew that Curtis hated the place and hated the posting. But this was a major story: get it right and Curtis had booked his passage to headquarters. Harris reckoned that was all Philip Curtis could think about.

The approach was backfiring on the superintendent, and backfiring badly. Butterfield, who had sneaked into the back of an impromptu press conference in the police station canteen that morning, had reported that the superintendent had floundered badly in the face of the journalists' questions, entirely because he had nothing to tell them about the progress of the inquiry. The reason he had nothing to say was because Jack Harris had deliberately told his superior nothing. Indeed, the inspector had spent the morning studiously avoiding the rampaging commander, suspecting that behind the cant and the bluster lay a man who was experiencing serious anxiety at such unprecedented happenings in his area. Harris was not about to help him out.

There was another reason for the inspector's reluctance to confide in his commander. Harris knew from long experience that word travelled fast in the tight-knit hill communities of the North Pennines. Harris had determined to keep his next moves from all but a few trusted confidantes, and Philip Curtis was not among them.

Now, shortly after nine, Harris was ensconced in his office, reviewing the case with Roberts and Butterfield; Scoot was curled up in a corner, taking a rest from all the excitement in the corridors. The office door was firmly shut. Sipping from his mug of tea, the DCI eyed Gillian Roberts for a moment. Harris knew her calmness and experience would be crucial in the hours to come. Alison Butterfield, surprised but delighted to be at the meeting, sat with eyes gleaming as she enjoyed being at the heart of her first major investigation. Harris had made an impulsive decision to invite her to attend: watching her go about her work, he had felt a quiet sense of satisfaction at the young officer's composure and had resolved to give her as much responsibility as she could handle. He sensed that he could trust her and that had suddenly become very important. Knowing that Matty Gallagher wanted away, and realistic enough to know that he could not block his application for ever, the inspector planned to recommend Butterfield for sergeant when his transfer was granted.

'So,' said Harris, looking expectantly at his officers, 'where exactly are we? Alison, how was Billy Dent's widow?'

'Didn't say much that we don't know. She said he was not much for talking.'

'He certainly wasn't,' said Harris, turning to Roberts. 'Gillian?'

'The roadblocks didn't pick anything up,' she said, glancing down at her notes. 'Couple of poachers, that's about it. The rabbits are in the freezer, if you're interested.'

'Thanks,' said Harris with a slight smile. 'I'm not surprised that they didn't turn up anything, mind. If this lot planned their way in, they planned their way out again. It's the first rule of special operations.'

Butterfield looked at him. Before he had gone to London, Matty Gallagher had commented that Harris was starting to talk about his Army days and both had agreed that the investigation seemed to be reawakening old instincts in the inspector. Butterfield glanced at Roberts: for the first time in a long time, they were beginning to see glimpses of the detective who had risen so rapidly up the ranks in his Manchester days.

'Maybe the reason the roadblocks did not stop anyone,' said Butterfield, 'was that the robbers were locals.

From what Edna Jessop said, it was an accident that the gun went off. Maybe it was a bungled job.'

'It's way out of any of the local bad lads' league,' said Roberts. 'Break into anything bigger than sheds and they get nose bleeds.'

'Which brings us back to Corbett and Garbutt,' said Butterfield.

Roberts nodded. 'They'd know how to stage a robbery,' she said. 'And Garbutt is still missing. Hasn't been home since last night. His wife is going frantic.'

The inspector's mobile phone rang.

'It's Matty,' said the sergeant's voice.

'Where are you?'

'Approaching Birmingham.'

'And chummy?'

'Three cars ahead of me.'

'Don't lose him,' said Harris.

'Don't worry, I have no intention of seeing your short and curlies, guv.'

'I'll not ask,' said Harris and replaced the phone in his pocket before looking across the desk at the two detectives.

'Ok, listen,' he said in a conspiratorial voice, turning to face the others, 'what I am about to say stays within these four walls. And that means that not even Curtis gets to hear about it. Understand?'

They nodded, startled by the intensity of his voice but before he could continue, there was a knock on the door as the superintendent walked in without waiting for a reply.

'I wonder if I could talk to the DCI on his own,' said Curtis quietly.

Disturbed by his grave expression, the others left the room without a word. Once they had gone, the superintendent sat down at the desk.

'We keep missing each other, Jack,' he said, eying the DCI keenly.

'Been busy.'

'Any leads?'

'Bits and pieces. Plenty of maybes. Nothing firm.' The DCI's reply was non-committal.

'I need something more than that.'

'When I have it, I'll let you know.'

'Is there nothing I can tell them?' The commander's voice sounded almost pleading. 'We're getting crucified in the media. Surely we fancy Ralph Corbett for this now?'

'Not quite that simple.'

'For God's sake, Jack!' exclaimed Curtis, a vein starting to throb on his neck. 'We need something more than that. I don't mind telling you that people are asking questions, people are asking questions at the very highest level.'

'Questions?'

'They are saying that you can't handle it. That Corbett was there under your nose all the time and that you did not see it.'

'It's a complex case,' said the DCI guardedly.

There was a pause for a few moments as the two men looked at each other.

'Maybe you should bring in some help,' said the superintendent.

'We'll be ok. Matty will be back later today – we've had to let Gerald Hopson go so he's not needed down there.'

'Another dead-end,' groaned Curtis, raising his eyes to the ceiling. 'We have to do something, Jack.'

'Ok, ok, I admit it, we could do with a little more help. Maybe a couple of DCs from Central. Maybe you could square it with Phil Jacques.'

'Actually, I was thinking of someone a little more senior than that.'

'Were you now?' said the DCI evenly. 'Like who?'

'A DCI maybe.'

'But I'm a DCI.'

'It would just be to help you out for a day or two. No big deal.'

'And is this your crappy idea or has it come from headquarters?' asked Harris, looking hard at the superintendent.

'I can make it official through headquarters if you want,' said the superintendent, managing a nervous smile as he surveyed the inspector's darkening demeanour and trying hard to sound a little more conciliatory. 'Don't look like that, I'm just trying to help. I mean, this is a massive inquiry now and I just think it might be too much for you on your own, particularly considering…'

He hesitated.

'Considering what?' asked Harris.

'I'm hearing things, Jack.'

'Things? What things?'

'That you might be too close to this one.'

'Ralph Corbett may have been a friend but as far as that goes, it does not make a difference and as far Davy Garbutt, we were never fr…'

'I wasn't thinking of them.'

The superintendent's words seemed to hang in the air for a few seconds.

'Then who were you thinking about?' asked the inspector.

'Ella Reynolds.'

'What about her?'

Curtis stared down at the desk.

'Well?' said Harris, his voice hard-edged now. 'Come on, spit it out. What about Ella Reynolds?'

'Look, this is not easy for either of us,' said the superintendent happily, 'but I would be neglecting my duty if I did not act when I heard things. Did you sleep with her?'

'And who told you that I did?'

'Who does not matter. What matters is that I need to know if it's true because if it is, the inquiry is compromised and I have to think about bringing someone else in. Michael Graham is happy to come in and help you out. Distance you from Reynolds.'

'I'll bet he is,' said Harris darkly, 'he's been after this job for years. And there's no prizes for guessing who's been whispering in daddy's ear about me. Well, I suggest that young Robbie Graham keeps his mouth shut in future. There have already been too many loose tongues. You, of all people, should know that.'

Curtis looked at him uncertainly.

'What do you mean?' he asked.

'I do hear tell,' said Harris, his voice laced with quiet anger, 'that you were discussing the case with Michael in the pub at Halsey Bridge two nights ago. All very cosy, apparently.'

Curtis looked alarmed.

'Luckily,' said Harris, 'the person who overheard you came to me before telling anyone else – it's somewhat galling to find out from a barmaid that your divisional commander wants to replace you. And I am sure I do not have to tell you the implications if word had got out that you thought I had been sleeping around with a defence solicitor. Ella Reynolds would be laughing into her cocktail.'

Curtis opened his mouth to speak but Harris cut across him.

'So, for the benefit of the gossips, yes, Ella Reynolds did proposition me – according to the Met lads, it's one of her favourite tricks – but no, I did not sleep with her.'

'I am glad to hear that,' said Curtis, embarrassed by the inspector's comments but trying to retain his dignity. 'Look, I didn't mean any harm by... that is... you know how it is... headquarters is getting a bit twitchy about...'

His voice tailed off as he watched Harris pick up a pen from the desk and twirl it round in his fingers. Curtis found himself mesmerised by the scene, watching uneasily, almost as if fearing that the inspector might suddenly lunge across the table and plunge the pen into his chest.

'Have you ever heard of Lenny Jarman?' asked Harris at length, replacing the pen on the desk.

'No.' The question caught Curtis by surprise.

'Ooh, he was a bad lad, was Lenny Jarman,' said Harris, standing up and walking over to the window. 'He and his gang killed four people over a five-week period in Manchester a few years back. A drugs turf war.'

He returned to sit at his desk and began twirling the pen round again.

'They all went away for long stretches,' said the inspector, 'but it took a real effort because for weeks not one eyewitness dared speak out and things were not helped by the media screaming for arrests, community leaders shouting off their mouths and even some senior police officers questioning whether the investigating team was up to the job, behind their backs, of course. Can you believe that? Never happen here.'

Curtis glanced down at the desk.

'In the end,' continued Harris, 'the trial judge said what a well-run inquiry it had been. Indeed, all the officers involved ended up with commendations. Do you know who ran that inquiry, Philip? Do you?'

Curtis shook his head, startled by the inspector's use of his Christian name – it was the first time it had ever happened. Somehow it sounded menacing.

'I ran it,' said Harris fiercely, leaning forward and jabbing the pen into the desk. 'I ran it, Philip, so don't tell me I can't handle something like this. Don't you ever do that.'

'No need to be so aggressive,' said Curtis defensively, trying to conceal the tremor in his voice. 'I just need to make sure that we have got this right.'

'Yeah, we don't want you to look stupid in front of the cameras,' snapped Harris. 'That would put the kybosh on your little plan for a nice desk and a pretty pot plant at headquarters, wouldn't it?'

The two men stared at each other in silence for a few moments. The superintendent looked as if he was about to say something then shrugged and stood up.

'Have it your way,' he said and walked to the door. 'But I warn you, Jack, headquarters wants to see this wrapped up as soon as possible.'

'Headquarters,' said the inspector as Curtis left the room, 'will get it wrapped up when I am ready.'

After the superintendent had departed, Harris sat in his office for a few moments, staring out of the window. The superintendent's question about Ella Reynolds had not taken him by surprise and he began wondering idly about who could have been gossiping about it. Who knew that she had propositioned him? Alison Butterfield, he was sure she knew. Matty Gallagher, he suspected. Gillian Roberts, he was pretty sure she knew. But the truth, and Jack Harris knew it, was that everyone at the police station had heard the rumours. He allowed himself a slight smile. You could always rely on the bush telegraph, he thought. Harris was certain that Ella Reynolds had been depending on it as well: discredit the investigating officer and the case was automatically weakened. Raine had warned him that that was her way of working because she knew how the rumours that ensued could derail an inquiry. She was a formidable adversary, thought Harris, but if you knew how to play the game…

He reached for his mobile phone and dialled a number.

'Well?' he said.

'Got everything you need,' said Leckie's voice at the other end.

'How did you manage that? I thought you said there was no paper trail because nothing was proved.'

'I managed to track down one of our retired officers. He confirmed the lot.'

'That's another pint I owe you.'

'I'll be able to open a pub at this rate.'

When Leckie had rung off, the inspector made another call.

'It's Harris,' he said. 'Tell me I'm right.'

'You are right,' said a voice, the pathologist unable to conceal his amazement, 'but I have no idea how you knew.'

'I'll tell you when I come down.'

* * *

An hour later, the inspector and Alison Butterfield walked into the mortuary room at Roxham Hospital and stood watching the pathologist examining the charred corpse of the body found in Ralph Corbett's office. The pathologist glanced up as they entered.

'So go on,' he said, with a disbelieving shake of the head, 'tell me how you knew. It's taken me three hours to be absolutely certain.'

'Knew the moment I saw him sitting there that something was wrong.'

'It certainly was,' nodded the pathologist, pointing to the dead man's neck. 'Oh, before we come to the vexed issue of his identity, for the record I reckon that he was killed before the blaze started.'

'That's a blessing,' said Harris. 'The fire boys reckon an accelerant had been poured over him – presumably to make it more difficult to confirm his identity.'

'That would certainly fit in with the extent of his injuries. Thankfully, he would seem to have been dead before it happened.'

'Is someone going to tell me what the hell you are talking about?' asked a bewildered Butterfield, glancing first at the pathologist then at the chief inspector. 'What do you mean the vexed issue of his identity?'

'In a minute,' said Harris. 'First I need to know how the good doctor knows I am right.'

'Your Mr Corbett had a bad knee, I think?'

'Yeah,' said Harris. 'Damaged it trying to arrest a burglar a few years back. Walked with a bad limp.'

'Scar tissue,' nodded the pathologist, wiping his hands and walking over to a desk where he opened the drawer and withdrew a document which he held up. 'Whoever did the operation did a pretty amateurish job, I'm afraid to say. Typical NHS, if you ask me. Anyway, that does not matter, what does matter is that there is no sign of this man having gone through anything like that.'

'You are surely not saying that this is not Ralph Corbett?' asked Butterfield, gazing at the corpse. 'I mean, I saw them bring him out of the cabin.'

'You saw someone,' said the pathologist, replacing the document in the drawer and returning to survey the charred corpse, 'but not Ralph Corbett.'

Butterfield whirled round to face the chief inspector.

'You keep this a secret,' said Harris with a sudden fierceness. 'If word gets out about this then it could screw everything up. As far as anyone knows, Ralph Corbett is dead. Understand?'

Butterfield nodded dumbly then looked back at the body.

'So, if it's not Ralph Corbett then who is it?' she asked.

'That's the bit I'm not sure about,' said Harris.

'Then maybe I can help,' said the pathologist, walking over to a tray on the side-bench and fishing out a medallion. 'I found this round his neck. Not sure if it assists your inquiries or not.'

'What is it?' asked Butterfield as the pathologist held it up to the light.

'It's a regimental medallion and I've seen it before,' said Jack Harris quietly before looking down at the body. 'Ladies and gentlemen, meet Geordie Carroll.'

And the watcher watched no more.

* * *

Davy Garbutt was driving through one of the division's southern villages when the traffic ground to a halt. He sat in his car for a few moments, drumming his fingers nervously on the steering wheel, when he noticed in his rear view mirror the figure of Gillian Roberts walking along the pavement towards him. With an alarmed cry, Garbutt leapt from the car only to find the path blocked by a couple of uniformed officers.

'Sorry, Davy,' said one of them uncomfortably. 'DCI's orders.'

Garbutt turned and waited for DI Roberts to arrive.

* * *

As Harris and Butterfield were walking across the hospital car park after their meeting with the pathologist, the inspector's mobile phone rang.

'Harris,' he said.

'It's Bob,' said the search and rescue team leader. 'We've got an eyeball on Ralph Corbett – Mike Ganton and one of the other lads have just seen him parking up at the bottom of Dead Hill. He's alone. What do you want them to do?'

'Keep their distance. He's dangerous.'

'Come on,' said Crowther. 'This is Ralph Corbett we are talking about. I mean, you know what he's like.'

'I thought I did,' said Harris as he paused to let a car drive past on its way out of the car park. 'Just keep them well back. I'm on my way.'

'Ok, Hawk,' said Crowther, 'you know best.'

Harris made another call.

'Matty, lad, where are you?' he asked.

'Approaching Manchester – he's parked up in a service station car park. Looks like this is where the meet will be.'

'Stick with him. Leckie's expecting your call. He'll rustle up some troops for you.'

The chief inspector replaced the phone in his pocket and produced his car keys.

'Are you going to tell me what this is about?' asked Butterfield.

'I think,' said Harris, unlocking the door and swinging himself into the drivers' seat, 'that Matty was right. I think it is about Jimmy Roscoe.'

* * *

Fifty minutes later, he and the detective constable pulled up at the entrance to the animal sanctuary. Parking the Land Rover in the road, they walked along the paths, still able to smell the stale smell of smoke on the heavy afternoon air. Harris stopped and surveyed the wrecked Portacabin for a few moments.

'Such a waste,' he said with a shake of the head, 'such a waste. Come on, Constable, let's get this over with.'

They walked up to the house and rang the front door bell. Standing there waiting for a reply, Harris looked back down across the animal sanctuary and shook his head again.

'What will happen to all the animals?' he said. 'Who will look after them now?'

'You never change,' replied the constable.

They heard the sound of someone walking down the hall and Maureen Corbett opened the door. Harris glanced past her and noticed a couple of suitcases.

'Going somewhere?' he asked.

'No, I'm just…' Her voice tailed off when saw the expression on his face.

The inspector nodded at Butterfield.

'Maureen Corbett,' said the constable, 'I am arresting you as an accessory to the murder of George Carroll.'

Chapter fourteen

Late afternoon sunlight dappled the landscape as Harris stood in the car park and stared up at Dead Hill. Behind him were ranged police officers and members of the mountain search and rescue team, the only sound the low murmur of their voices and the clink of metal as they checked and re-checked their equipment before embarking on the climb up the slopes. Jack Harris let his eyes range across the hills, trying to remember what it felt like when they were *his* hills, his sanctuary. Perhaps, he thought as his gaze reached the summit and he imagined the fells stretching away into the distance, this is where Ralph Corbett was now confronting his own demons.

Bob Crowther walked over.

'Just had Mike Ganton on,' he said. 'He says that Corbett is in Metcalfe's Cottage. Don't worry, he hasn't clocked them. They are pretending to be a couple of walkers.'

'They have done a brilliant job,' said Harris, patting Crowther on the shoulder. 'Pass the word on, will you?'

'Sure, but what's the plan, Hawk? I mean, it will take us ages to get up there.'

'Maybe not.'

'But...'

Crowther's voice stilled in his throat as he heard the distant clatter of rotor blades and he turned round to see the dark shape of a military assault helicopter approaching them along the valley.

'Bloody hell?' he exclaimed. 'How did you get one of those?'

'Standard police issue,' grinned Harris. 'Or it is when an old mate of yours gets to run an airbase.'

'You never cease to amaze,' said Crowther with a disbelieving shake of the head. 'But it won't be able to land up on the fells, you know. Even if he finds a flat area, it's far too wet.'

'Who said anything about landing?' said Harris and waved his arms at the approaching helicopter. 'Start taking your lads up, I have a feeling we may need them.'

Five minutes later, the chief inspector, Butterfield and two uniformed constables were sitting in the back of the helicopter as it rose once more into the air and scaled the side of Dead Hill. The inspector, eyes gleaming as he relished the sensation, looked down at the copse and the chuckling beck disappearing rapidly beneath. He glanced across at Butterfield, who was sitting opposite him, knuckles glowing white as she clung on to her seat.

'Ever been in one of these?' shouted Harris over the noise.

'I'm a farmer's daughter from Yarrowby,' she yelled back. 'What do you think?'

'Last time I was in a chopper,' yelled Harris, peering out as the machine crested the top of the hill and started out across the fells, 'we were being dropped behind the lines in Kuwait. Bloody brilliant, it was!'

Butterfield saw an expression she had never seen on his face before, an excitement, a sense that Jack Harris was where he was supposed to be. But she did not let her thoughts focus on him for long because the helicopter suddenly dipped and she cried out and clung onto her seat even tighter. The inspector roared with laughter and reached into his pocket as his mobile phone rang.

'Harris,' shouted the inspector.

'Where the hell are you!' yelled Gallagher down the phone.

'You wouldn't believe it if I told you. What's happening?'

'He's here – so are the cavalry. What do you want us to do?'

'Bring it to an end,' said Harris.

* * *

Sitting in the service station car park, Gallagher pocketed his phone and glanced over at the officer in the passenger seat.

'Showtime?' asked Leckie.

'Showtime,' said Gallagher.

The officers got out of the car and walked towards the motel. Two plain-clothes officers got out of a nearby patrol car and fell into step.

'Round the back,' said Gallagher, gesturing to the rear of the motel. 'They might try to get out of the window.'

After waiting for the officers to disappear from view, Gallagher and Leckie walked through reception.

'A bloke came in five minutes ago,' said Gallagher, flashing his ID at the startled receptionist. 'Visiting a chap who booked a room. Where are they?'

'Room seventeen,' said the young girl. 'It's on the first floor.'

The two officers walked in silence up the stairs and scanned the deserted corridor.

'Third on the right,' said the sergeant, pointing at one of the doors.

They moved quietly and Gallagher hesitated for a moment and looked at Leckie. The constable nodded and Gallagher knocked loud on the door, the noise reverberating along the corridor.

'Who is it?' asked a voice.

'Police!'

There was a few moments' silence then the door opened and Gallagher stared into the face of Gerald Hopson. Standing behind him was a startled Robert de Luca.

'Fancy meeting you here,' said Gallagher.

* * *

As the helicopter started to swoop low over the fells, Harris scanned the moors with his binoculars. After a few moments, he cried out and pointed to two figures dressed in orange, who were crouching behind a rock. One of them raised an arm and pointed towards a small cottage a few hundred metres away.

'Metcalfe's!' shouted Harris to Butterfield and tapped the pilot on the shoulder. 'Put us down as near as you can, will you?'

The pilot nodded and the helicopter started to dip. For a few moments, it hovered a few feet over the boggy moorland and Harris glanced at Butterfield, who gawped at him.

'Surely you are not serious?' she exclaimed.

'It's easy,' grinned Harris. 'Just roll up like a ball.'

Then he was gone, falling through the air to hit the heather and roll over before bouncing back to his feet. He gestured to Butterfield, who hesitated then took a deep breath and hurled herself out of the door. Seconds later, she was down, hitting the ground so hard that it drove the breath from her body. Harris hauled her to her feet and for a few moments, she leaned against him, coughing and spluttering as she tried to regain her senses.

'You'd never make a Para,' he said.

Butterfield saw that the two uniforms had made the jump as well and that Mike Ganton and his fellow rescue team member were running towards them.

'He's still in there,' shouted Ganton, gesturing at Metcalfe's. 'Been in there for ages. God knows what he's doing.'

'Time to find out,' said Harris, glancing up as the helicopter pilot gave the thumbs up and angled his machine away across the fells.

The group started to walk across the moor towards the little stone cottage, which had been used as a refuge for stranded walkers and shepherds for many generations. As they neared it, the door flew open and smoke billowed out into the chill afternoon air, followed by a flash of flame. Harris reacted first, sprinting across the moors, his feet crashing through the heather as he saw a figure run out of the building. Although he was partially obscured by the smoke, the man was still recognisable to the inspector as Ralph Corbett. Harris could see that he was clutching a petrol can.

'Ralph!' shouted Harris.

'You're too late,' said Corbett, turning to face him with a crooked smile. 'I've destroyed the evidence.'

'What evidence?' asked Harris, slowing down and starting to walk towards him.

'That's where we killed Jimmy Roscoe,' said Corbett, gesturing to the blazing building.

As Harris watched, the roof started to buckle and some of the slates gave way, sending the flames dancing with renewed vigour.

'But now you can't prove it,' added Corbett with a strange laugh.

'Come on,' said the inspector, holding out a hand. 'It's time to end it, Ralph. It's gone too far. Too many people have died.'

Harris saw that Corbett had started to cry.

'I did not mean it to be like this,' he said. 'Just Paul de Luca. That was the deal. Just Paul de Luca. It just got out of hand.'

There was a dull thud then a splintering sound from the cottage as one of the windows cracked then shattered, sending shards of glass flying through the air. Harris reacted too slowly and a piece of glass caught him in the face, ripping its way through flesh and sending him staggering backwards, clutching his cheek. Corbett seized the moment and started to run across the moor. One of the uniformed officers sprinted past Harris, who struggled to his feet, blood pouring from his wound. As the uniformed officer gained on Corbett, he spun round and lashed out with the petrol can, catching the constable full in the face, sending him crashing backwards with a squeal of agony. Harris was helped to his feet by the other uniformed officer and together they ran after the fleeing Corbett. Glancing down, they saw the prostrate constable clutching his fractured jaw, which was already bulging alarmingly.

'Enough, Ralph,' shouted Harris as Corbett drew away from them. 'There's nowhere to run! Give it up!'

Corbett stopped, surveyed the endless moors stretching to the horizon, and turned to face his old friend.

'I can't,' he said, his voice shaking slightly.

'The doctor says you are ill,' said the inspector, holding out a hand. 'We'll tell that to the court, they might be lenient. There are people who can help you.'

'A loony bin!' Corbett laughed darkly. 'Can you really see me with all those nutters? No thanks, Jack.'

He started to walk away then stopped as something on the ground caught his eye. The inspector followed his gaze and stiffened as he realised that Corbett was within feet of a hole in the ground, partially concealed beneath the bracken. The inspector held up a hand as Butterfield and the uniformed officer edged forwards.

'Do you know what that is?' he murmured.

Butterfield shook her head.

'It's Blind Man's Level,' whispered Ganton, joining them. 'It's where eight lead miners died when a tunnel collapsed in 1843. See, there's a little cairn over there.'

He pointed to a small pile of stones.

'It's why they call it Dead Hill,' said Harris.

'Do you know how far this goes down?' asked Corbett, pointing to the hole with a strange smile.

'They say it has no bottom,' said Harris, trying to remain calm as Corbett moved his feet closer to the edge. 'Come on Ralph... please.'

Corbett shook his head.

'They never found the bodies,' he said. 'You never found Jimmy either. A fine way for it to end, really.'

And he vanished into the earth without a sound.

Chapter fifteen

Jack Harris pushed his way into the interview room and surveyed the hunched figure of Maureen Corbett sitting at the table. Butterfield glanced up at the inspector and shook her head sadly. Harris looked up at the wall clock: 10:30pm. Suddenly he felt very tired and the gash on his face, now stitched up, was throbbing remorselessly. It seemed to be a few moments before Maureen noticed that Harris had entered the room but when she did, she lifted a tear-stained face to him, hope breaking through the despair. The look faded as she saw the inspector's grim expression.

'I'm sorry, Maureen,' he said. 'We've had to call in a specialist mine rescue team but they say it is too dangerous to go down there.'

'But is there not a chance that he is still alive?' she asked, eyes filled with hope.

'They've put listening and thermal detection equipment down there and they're pretty sure he's gone,' and he looked at her sadly. 'I'm sorry, Maureen.'

Her unearthly wail was to stay with both detectives for many years to come. It was the sound of despair, of black, hopeless despair, and now her tears came freely.

Tears that she had restrained for so many hours, tears that had been held back as long as there was hope, tears that now coursed down her cheeks. Neither Harris or Butterfield could fail to be moved by them and the inspector closed his eyes and leaned his head against the wall. Eventually, he sat down at the table.

'Maureen,' he said softly. 'We have to know the truth.'

She nodded dumbly and dabbed moist eyes with a handkerchief.

'Tell me about the beginning,' said the inspector. 'Why did Ralph kill Jimmy Roscoe?'

'It wasn't him alone,' she said quickly, her voice seeming to gather strength at the suggestion. 'And it was an accident. They did not mean to kill him. That's what he said.'

'Who's they?'

'Garry Roscoe. The de Lucas. Gerald Hopson was there as well.'

'How come Ralph knew him?'

'The de Lucas introduced them. Ralph said he handled the money side of things for them.'

'Why did Ralph get involved, for God's sake?' asked Harris. 'I mean, a copper, Maureen, a copper. Surely he knew the risk he was taking?'

Maureen took a deep breath and composed herself, dabbing at her eyes with a handkerchief.

'Did you know he had a gambling problem, Jack?' she asked.

'I knew he liked the odd flutter.'

'It was more than that.' She shook her head. 'By the time we were living in Liverpool, it had got really bad. We had everything but he threw it all away. He lost thousands. I only found out when we got a letter saying the building society was threatening to repossess the house. He'd hidden it from me for so long.'

Her voice tailed off.

'You think you know someone,' she said quietly.

Harris nodded. 'You do,' he said. 'So, what happened?'

'Paul de Luca heard about it somehow.' There was a momentary fire in her eyes. 'He was an evil, evil man. A parasite. He approached Ralph, said he knew Ralph was desperate for cash and that the gang would pay him for inside information.'

'I still can't believe it,' said Harris. 'I mean, Ralph was as straight as they came.'

'Everyone has their price, Jack. Besides, it saved the house. Ralph said that was all that mattered. He said he would do anything to ensure that me and the kids weren't thrown out onto the streets. He said he was not hurting anyone, just tipping the gang off about where the rich people garaged their cars. He said the owners could claim it back on the insurance. A victimless crime, he said.'

'There's no such thing,' said Harris. 'So, what happened then?'

'The police raided the workshop one night and arrested the Roscoes. They kept quiet about the involvement of the others and Garry said that meant Ralph owed them a favour. When he was released, Garry suggested that they start up again with Ralph providing the information as before.'

'And did he?'

'Ralph had no option, we were even deeper in debt than before. The bailiffs had been round again and we'd had a final warning from the building society. We tried to keep it from the kids but they worked out that something was wrong – it tore the family apart. Starting up again was the answer to our problems.'

'But Jimmy Roscoe refused to get involved again?' said Harris.

She nodded.

'They tried to make him change his mind. Followed him out onto the hills one day. Took him to Metcalfe's Cottage.'

'So, who killed Jimmy?' asked the inspector.

She shrugged.

'Ralph never said but I always had the idea that it was Garry. They agreed to keep what had happened a secret. Robert de Luca said that he did not want to be involved any more – he was terrified by what had happened. Ralph worried about it for years. Said he should torch Metcalfe's to get rid of the evidence, but as time went on, he relaxed a little. No one ever suspected what had happened – everyone just said Jimmy had fallen down a mine shaft.'

'His mother never believed that,' said Harris.

'Poor woman,' said Maureen quietly.

'So, what happened after the murder?' asked Butterfield.

'Ralph kept feeding them information for a few years. There was one nasty moment when he had to arrest Paul during a raid but he put a word in for him afterwards. I don't think anyone ever suspected the reason.'

'Not sure that's true,' said Harris. 'Ralph was the subject of an undercover investigation by Merseyside's complaints unit.'

'Ralph never knew that.' She looked shocked.

'No one did. It was discontinued for lack of evidence. We only found out because one of my friends happens to know the officer who ran it.'

The inspector's thoughts turned to Leckie: he'd be buying him pints for ever.

'Perhaps,' said Maureen, 'bringing it out into the open might have been the best thing for everyone. Mind, for years it looked like it had gone away. When Ralph was transferred up here, Paul de Luca said he was not prepared to nick cars in an area where everyone knew him. We hadn't heard from any of them for years.'

'Until word got round that Paul de Luca had turned informant?' said Harris.

'Robert de Luca rang Ralph one night. He was terrified that it would all come out. They both were. And

Hopson was beside himself apparently. They were scared that Paul would say who killed Jimmy.'

'So they killed Paul to keep him quiet?'

She nodded.

'Presumably, by tricking him into coming up here for the eagle eggs?' said Harris.

'It was Hopson's idea to stage the accident. Roped in Rawmarsh. Said he would pay him to do it.'

'So Rawmarsh was in on it.'

'He hated the idea that Paul was a grass.'

'Which he wasn't,' said Harris. 'God knows where the rumour came from but it wasn't true.'

She digested the information for a few moments then shook her head.

'What a mess,' she said.

'So how did they kill Paul?' asked Harris.

'Persuaded him to meet them up there then made it look like he had fallen getting the eggs. Ralph said Eddy Rawmarsh delivered the blow that killed him. Hopson didn't do anything. They knew you'd probably spot them but they reckoned you would assume it was an accident. And, good as gold, you turned up.' She gave a slight smile. 'You and your birds, Jack.'

'Then what happened?' asked Harris, ignoring the comment.

'When you announced that it was murder, they panicked. Ralph was about to give himself up but then word spread about your interest in Jimmy Roscoe. Ralph came up with the idea of making out that Garry killed Paul. He pretended that the break-ins were Garry's doing.'

'So who really did them?' asked Butterfield.

Maureen shrugged.

'Could have been anyone,' she said. 'Ralph always reckoned it was to do with the trouble with those teenagers in the market place.'

'And the assault on Ralph?' asked Harris. 'I assume that was faked?'

'I did that.' She gave a little smile. 'Hit him on the head with a shovel. Ralph said he deserved it.'

'Surely Ralph knew he could not get away with it,' said Butterfield.

'He reckoned that with him and Davy Garbutt saying they had seen Garry, you might believe it.'

'How come Garbutt was involved?'

'Ralph and Davy had been friends for years. Davy did not need much persuading to help an old friend out. Anything for money. Besides, he had an idea what had happened to Jimmy because Ralph was the one who told him to drop the case at the time.'

'But surely they knew we'd work it out eventually,' said Harris.

'Ralph said that even if you did, it would still buy us time. He was delighted when you went down to London. He reckoned then there was no way anyone would take Garry Roscoe's word over a couple of ex-coppers and he said that Garry could not say anything without incriminating himself.'

'Except Garry had actually been under surveillance by the Met for weeks,' said Harris. 'They knew he had not left London.'

'The best laid plans,' she said.

'And what was the plan?' asked Harris, his mind going back to the suitcases in the hall. 'Escape?'

'We planned to let things die for a few days then leave the country – say we needed a break from the stress. Even if people did start to suspect, Ralph reckoned you would vouch for him anyway. Everyone knows you look after your friends, Jack. It was a gamble. Ralph never was a good gambler.'

There was silence for a few moments as Harris tried to digest all that he was hearing.

'And Billy Dent?' asked Harris. 'Where does he fit in with things?'

'Billy saw him near the quarry on the day of the murder. Ralph paid him to say he had seen Garry Roscoe instead.'

'So why kill him?'

'Billy had a change of mind. Said he did not like lying to you, threatened to say what he knew. Ralph reckoned a botched robbery would throw you off the scent for a little while.'

'So who was the other man at Jessop's farmhouse when Billy was shot?' asked Harris. 'Davy Garbutt, I assume?'

'Yes, but Ralph fired the shot.'

'What the hell was he thinking?' murmured Harris.

'Not sure he was thinking. He had lost it by then. The doctor diagnosed him with depression two years ago but Ralph had stopped taking his tablets. Said he'd had enough of doctors to last him a lifetime. I couldn't talk to him at the end, he was acting really strangely.'

She started to sob again. As the detectives waited until she had composed herself, Butterfield's mind went back to her conversations with Corbett, to the dirty enclosures and the tools strewn across the shed floor. It all made sense now. If only, she thought, if only she had noticed the danger signs. But as Harris was always saying to his officers, all crimes are solved by DI Hindsight.

'And Geordie Carroll. Why kill him?'

'Pure bad luck. Ralph had heard that the eagle watchpoint would be unmanned that morning because one of the group couldn't make it. However, unbeknownst to Ralph, Geordie turned up anyway. He came to see Ralph afterward and said he had already told your sergeant that Rawmarsh and Hopson were in the quarry with de Luca. Carroll said he had been watching your investigation and that all he had to do was reveal everything he knew about what happened and the game was up. Demanded money to keep quiet. Ralph was terrified.'

'But why kill him – couldn't you just pay him off?'

'We hadn't got the money to pay him,' said Maureen with a dry laugh. 'Typical Ralph. After they had killed Billy Dent, he and Davy came back to the house and Geordie turned up, after his cash. There was a row, Ralph hit him, knocked him out. We panicked and Ralph started the fire. Hoped you would think it was him that had died.'

'Then what?'

'Ralph went up to Metcalfe's Cottage – said he had to burn the evidence about Jimmy. I told him not to but he had become obsessed with it by then. When he had done it, he was going to go with me to Manchester Airport. Gerald Hopson and Robert de Luca were going to meet us at a motel. Hopson had got hold of some false passports. Davy Garbutt was going to lie low and follow in a few days.'

There was silence in the interview room for a few moments as the detectives tried to take in all that they had been told.

'But why kill Rawmarsh and Hadleigh?' asked Harris eventually.

'That's the strange thing,' said Maureen with an odd smile. 'Ralph didn't.'

* * *

Harris left the room and walked into the CID room to see Matty Gallagher, sitting with his feet up as he drank a cup of coffee.

'Come on,' said Harris wearily, 'let's get this wrapped up.'

They walked along to Interview Room One and entered to see Robert de Luca sitting alongside the duty solicitor.

'What would your father think?' said Harris, sitting down as de Luca turned heavy eyes on them. 'Just what would your father think?'

De Luca said nothing.

'What was it you said to me?' asked Harris. 'There comes a time when a man has to choose the path down which he will walk. I guess you chose yours.'

'I guess I did.'

'I assume all those business trips abroad were bringing in cars for the gang?'

'They were.'

'But I thought you had gone straight.'

Robert shrugged. 'The garage was about to go bust. I said I'd do a couple of runs for them and it went from there. It went against the grain – you know how I detested the way Paul had turned out.'

Harris said nothing.

'Can I ask how you tied me in to it?' asked de Luca.

'Garry got careless – we found out about his phone calls to you.'

'He never was the brightest,' said de Luca. 'And Jimmy, how did you know I was there when Garry killed him?'

'Worked it backwards. When I put the truth to Edith Roscoe, she admitted it all. She saw you in the car the day Jimmy and Garry had their fight. She never told anyone because she wanted to protect you. Said you and Jimmy were like brothers.'

'Some brother,' laughed de Luca darkly, then turned haunted eyes on the inspector. 'I had no idea Garry was going to kill him. You have to believe me.'

'And Paul?' asked Harris. 'Did you want him to die?'

'There was no alternative,' said de Luca. 'When I heard that he was planning to turn into a police informant, I could not afford everything coming out. If I went inside, the business would fold and my kids would be on the street. There was no way I was going to let him tear my family apart. He'd already done enough damage.'

'Trouble is, he wasn't going to tell us anything,' said Harris, standing up and walking towards the door. 'Your secret was as safe with him as it ever was.'

De Luca stared at him.

'Like you said,' added the inspector. 'It's about the paths that we choose.'

* * *

It was almost eleven when Gallagher walked into the inspector's office. Harris was staring out of the window into the darkness of the night.

'She's here,' said the sergeant.

The inspector got up and followed him into the corridor. Before they reached the interview room, he stopped.

'You've done good work on this, Matty lad,' he said. 'Really good work.'

'Thank you.'

'I'll recommend that Curtis gives you that transfer if you like.'

Gallagher considered the comment for a few moments.

'Yeah, I've been thinking about that,' he said, 'I might hold off for a while. If that's ok with you. Sheep aren't that bad once you get to know them.'

'There's some communities up here where that comment might be construed the wrong way,' said Harris, patting him on the shoulder. 'Come on, sunshine, let's wrap this thing up.'

The detectives walked into the interview room and, after they had taken their seats, Harris surveyed Ella Reynolds for a few moments.

'Hello, Jack,' she said with a smile. 'Long time, no see.'

'Indeed.' There was no warmth in his voice.

'Might I ask where my client is?'

'Gerald Hopson is in his cell – we'll interview him tomorrow morning. But this is not about him.'

She looked at him uneasily, her smile banished.

'What do you mean?'

'How long had William Hadleigh known what you were doing?'

'I have no idea what you are talking about,' she said but she seemed taken aback by the question.

'How long had he known that you were helping Gerry Hopson launder money for a couple of the London gangs?'

'No comment,' she said icily.

'That doesn't work in a backwater like this,' said Harris. 'You are going to be charged with murder anyway.'

'Murdering whom?' she said, laughing out loud.

'We believe that you murdered William Hadleigh and Eddy Rawmarsh.'

'I very much doubt you'll get that to stick in court. Or get it past the CPS, for that matter.'

'Depends how long you think Gerald Hopson can keep his gob shut without you sitting by his side,' replied Harris. 'All we really need from you is to know when Hadleigh found out about your little scam?'

She thought for a moment.

'Ok,' she said eventually. 'Gerry told him on their second night here, in the bar of that nasty little pub they stayed at after you released them the first time,' said Reynolds, her voice suddenly infused with anger. 'I mean, how stupid is that? We had a really good thing going then next thing I know, that little shit Hadleigh is trying to blackmail me. Said he would tell you about it if I didn't pay him.'

'So you cut his brakes?' asked Gallagher.

'Easy to get someone to do something like that, Sergeant.' She smiled slightly. 'I would like to think that we did it with a touch of elegance.'

'Jesus,' said Harris, shaking his head in disbelief.

'I thought that you would link it to the other crimes, assume that someone had it in for Eddy Rawmarsh because of what happened to Paul de Luca. Oh, don't look like that, Jack. I had no option. Can you imagine what would happen to an attractive woman like me in prison?'

'I guess now you'll be able to find out,' said Gallagher.

'Oh, I don't think so,' said Reynolds. 'I'll refuse to sign a statement, deny I ever admitted anything, and no jury in the land would convict me. They never convict attractive women.' She winked at the sergeant. 'And it's amazing what a good lawyer can do.'

* * *

It was midnight when Jack Harris reached the cottage. Leaving Scoot in the Land Rover, he walked slowly to Number Nine Chapel Row and knocked lightly on the door. Edith Roscoe opened it and ushered him in.

'Sorry, it's so late,' said Harris, walking into the narrow little hallway.

'Fifteen years too late,' she said with a slight smile, showing him into the living room.

Harris nodded.

'Indeed,' he said and walked over to pick up the old school photograph from the little table.

For a few moments he scanned the faces, Paul de Luca, Robert, Jimmy Roscoe with that inane smile, himself with his glowering expression. How long ago it all seemed now.

'They're supposed to be the best years of your life,' he said at length, replacing the picture and turning back into the room.

'They were for Jimmy,' she said.

Harris looked at her in surprise.

'Really?'

'He adored you, Jack Harris.' She walked over and placed a hand gently on his arm. 'Said you always looked out for him.'

'I'm not sure…'

'You were a good boy then and you are a good boy now. Your father was so proud of you. So proud.'

Harris felt tears stinging his eyes.

'I'm sorry,' he said, fumbling for a handkerchief.

'About what? I suppose I always knew that the truth would come out in the end but the last thing I wanted was to see Robert go to jail. He was such a nice boy. Jimmy loved him like a brother. He was so much better than Garry ever was,' and she looked at him with fondness in her eyes. 'I know I should have told the police what I knew but all I wanted was for them to find my son, and you've done that for me.'

'Yes, but I can never bring him back.' Harris looked at her with a helpless expression. 'There's no way anyone will risk going down to find him. Mine rescue say it is far too dangerous.'

Edith hobbled over to the window and stared out at the dark shape of the hills.

'Perhaps they don't need to,' she said. 'Perhaps, my Jimmy is finally at peace.'

Epilogue

Jack Harris stood at the top of Dead Hill and stared out across the vast expanse of the fells, Scoot sitting beside him. As the inspector let his gaze wander, he noticed two dark specks in the distance, soaring high on the thermals. Harris lifted his binoculars to his eyes and smiled when he realised that they were the golden eagles.

'We never did find your eggs,' he said quietly. 'Well, there's always next year.'

And this is where he comes. The place where he finds peace. The place where his demons cease their chatter. The place where he is at one with his world. At least for a few snatched hours.

THE END

List of characters

Mike Ganton – deputy leader of the mountain rescue team
Graham Leckie – a uniformed constable with Greater Manchester Police
William Hadleigh – lawyer for Eddy Rawmarsh
Ella Reynolds – lawyer for Gerald Hopson
Barry Ramsden – local optician and parish councillor
Garry Roscoe – local villain whose brother Jimmy disappeared
Edith Roscoe – his mother
Ralph Corbett – runs animal rescue centre
Maureen Roscoe – his wife
Danny Raine – Metropolitan Police officer

If you enjoyed this book, please let others know by leaving a quick review on Amazon. Also, if you spot anything untoward in the paperback, get in touch. We strive for the best quality and appreciate reader feedback.

editor@thebookfolks.com

www.thebookfolks.com

Made in the USA
San Bernardino, CA
28 September 2017